PRAISE FOR THE NOVELS OF
#1 NEW YORK TIMES BESTSELLING AUTHOR
CHRISTIE RIDGWAY

"Emotional and powerful...everything a romance reader could hope for."

--Publishers Weekly (starred review)

"Ridgway's feel-good read, with its perfectly integrated, extremely hot, and well-crafted love scenes, is contemporary romance at its best."

--Booklist (starred review)

"This sexy page-turner [is] a stellar kick-off to Ridgway's latest humor-drenched series."

--Library Journal

"Equally passionate and emotional, this tale will quicken pulses and firmly tug on the heartstrings of readers across the globe. An excellent story that you hope won't ever end!"

--RT Book Reviews (Top Pick)

"Sexy, sassy, funny, and cool, this effervescent sizzler nicely launches Ridgway's new series and is a perfect pick-me-up for a summer's day."

--Library Journal

"Ridgway's latest addition to the Cabin Fever series is heartwarming and gives us hope that second chances are always within reach...This small-town sweet romance is perfect to r   ys endures the test of time

T Book Reviews

KNOX

7 Brides for 7 Brothers

CHRISTIE RIDGWAY

Printed in the United States of America

ISBN: 978-1-939286-28-4

Chapter 1

—⟶≫⧐⧎⧏⟵—

Knox Brannigan filled a pint glass with a local craft brew and wondered when the night before the new year had turned so damn lonely. Behind the long, scarred bar at The Wake, a popular watering hole in Santa Monica, California, with uncharacteristic detachment he worked on the next drink order and watched over the raucous crowd of merrymakers packing the place. The afternoon shift had decorated the walls and ceiling with sparkly banners and shiny streamers and other festive paraphernalia. At the center of each table sat a pile of silly hats and cardboard-and-tissue paper horns.

The patrons were decked out as well, the eclectic mix—from surfers and bikers to stockbrokers and systems analysts—displaying their best beach casual. Though December 31, some of the men wore shorts and all the women were wrapped in bright and skimpy dresses. It had hit 75 degrees on the sand earlier that afternoon and he had even seen a sunburn or two.

But the happy people in happy clothes didn't alleviate his personal gloom.

Co-owner Esteban Meza bustled up with a box of fresh booze from the storeroom and started restocking the mirror-backed glass shelves. "Crazy busy tonight, yeah?"

"Yeah." A half-deflated silver helium balloon declaring a limp "YOLO!" in bright red letters drifted past Knox, looking as dispirited as he was beginning to feel. He batted it away before grabbing up a bottle of chardonnay and a clean goblet. What the hell was wrong with him?

"What the hell is wrong with you?" Eban asked, echoing Knox's inner voice. "You're grimacing. Mr. Party doesn't grimace on his favorite holiday."

Mr. Party.

"Come on, smile." Eban leaned close to talk over the noise and ticked off on his fingers. "There's excellent hooch, revelers in the mood to celebrate and spend, not to mention all those kisses coming your way at midnight."

"Excellent hooch is a contradiction in terms," Knox replied absently, distracted by the unpleasant realization that kisses from a variety of pretty ladies didn't spark in him a single flash of interest. "Hooch means inferior alcohol, often homemade."

Eban stared. "Since when did Mr. Party become Mr. English Class?"

Hearing his own words, Knox shook himself. Good God. He sounded like the hundred-year-old dragon of an admin his dad had assigned to Knox during those miserable months he'd attempted working for Colin Brannigan, media mogul.

Would Mrs. Dole have retired now that Colin had passed four months before? Knox made a mental note to check on the curmudgeon. Sue him, but he had a secret soft spot for the mean old bat. Every birthday he sent her a box of her favorite candy along with one of the alliterative insults they'd so often traded. Even now he could hear her cackle "slothful scoundrel" in his inner ear.

"There's that cheery expression I want to see," Eban said now. "Recalling happy New Year's past?"

Knox forced his lips to keep smiling. "There was that time I crashed my three oldest brothers' party. It was the first time I saw bare breasts. It was my first taste of tequila. And for the very first time, I kissed a girl—French style."

Eban hooted appreciatively. "Any chance we're going to get any Brannigans to *this* party?"

"Nah. Here, Connie." He pushed a rum-and-Coke toward the barmaid and watched her set it on her tray and then wade into the throng of customers. "Gabe and Hunter are cozied up with their new honeys. I assume Luke and Lizzie are ushering in midnight with her teenage niece, Kaitlyn. I don't know what the other three are doing exactly." His poor mother Kathleen, determined to have a daughter, had ended up with seven sons instead—and then died from a car accident when her youngest boy was only four. Knox took a moment to wish his baby brother well. Finn, a naval aviator younger than he by two years, was currently flying fast planes over somewhere dangerous—and that flying was dangerous in itself. On the day they'd learned of Colin's death, Finn had barely saved his jet from crashing when the arresting cable on the carrier deck broke.

The YOLO! balloon drifted by again, its elevation another inch lower and Knox ignored it while reaching for a bottle of Bushmills 21, the single malt whiskey that had been his father's favorite. He poured himself a half-shot and tossed it back.

Swallowing, he noticed Eban scrutinizing him again. "What?"

"Are you thinking about your dad?"

Instead of answering his friend's question, Knox glanced at one of the big screen TVs across the room to check on the countdown clock. "If we're going to serve that champagne, you better get it out of the back cooler."

"It's natural to feel something, you know," Eban said, not moving a muscle. "First New Year's Eve without your old man in the world."

But that was the thing—Colin couldn't be the source of Knox's crappy state of mind. At first he'd gone numb when Aunt Claire had phoned to say that the patriarch of the family had died of a rare and fast-moving cancer. He hadn't wanted anyone to know about his illness until he was gone and his body cremated.

But by the next day Knox had made sense of it. Colin Brannigan had died as he'd lived—on his own terms. Knox and three of his brothers had toasted the old man a few days after that and he'd noted his siblings' anger and sadness over being kept in the dark about the illness, though he'd shrugged it off. *It is what it is*, he'd told them then. He'd accepted Colin's death as well as the manner of it.

But sometime since—perhaps the recent holidays were to blame—Knox had found himself dragged down by a dark mood he couldn't shake. Catching a glimpse of his reflection in the mirror behind the bar, he noted the frown on his face and remembered Colin shouting on the day of their last blow-up that had precipitated Knox walking away from his job. *You never take anything seriously!* his father had declared.

Knox met his own eyes in the glass, noting the flat expression in their darkness. "Satisfied now, Dad?" he murmured.

But he didn't have more time to brood about brooding as the action in the bar heated up, the revelers wanting their drinks refreshed before the ball dropped. When it did, the crowd went crazy as they kissed their neighbors and guzzled their beverages and finally danced to the Red Hot Chili Peppers' instrumental rendition of "Auld Lang Syne" that someone queued up on the state-of-the-art jukebox. That segued into a version Prince had recorded live and while guitars wailed, Knox turned away from the crowd to wipe down the counter behind him.

"Knox?"

The female voice made him stiffen. Despite Eban's promise, not one pair of lips had met Knox's at midnight or any of the minutes following. He'd deliberately stayed behind the bar to keep it that way. But now...

"Are you going to ignore an old friend?"

"Of course not." He turned to find Nina Ford, an ex he hadn't seen in months and months. Running his gaze over her, he noted she was still brunette, still built, and...

"You're engaged?" he asked, staring at the rock on the fourth finger of her left hand. Hard to miss, because she was displaying it for him like a jewelry model.

"Don't look so surprised!"

"I'm not. Not in the least." It was why they'd broken up after all. She'd wanted to deepen their relationship, take it to a new level, while he'd liked it strictly fun and games, thank you very much. *You never take anything seriously!*

Shrugging off that last thought, he stepped closer and grabbed her hand, giving it a quick squeeze. "Congratulations."

"That's for the groom-to-be," she corrected, putting on a prim expression. "I'm supposed to get best wishes."

"Then you shall have them," Knox said, smiling. The woman wore happiness like a new coat. It looked good on her. Great. "And a drink on the house. Is the fortunate fiancé around? I'll buy him one too."

"Thanks. A draft beer for Don. You know what I like."

"I make a mean Lemon Drop. One's coming right up."

Her smile made identical cute dimples pop on her cheeks, then her expression sobered. "Knox. I'm so sorry about your dad."

"Thanks. I got your card. That was nice of you." He passed her the Lemon Drop and went to work on the beer. "Not that I was surprised, you were always nice."

"But not the right nice."

"Not the right man," Knox amended, pointing to himself.

"You once told me you'd never been in love," Nina said, and sipped from her drink.

"Not even when I was nine, the age you said you were when you had that big crush on your swimming coach."

"Ah, Jericho," she said, sending her eyes heavenward. "He was dreamy."

Knox laughed and slid the beer her way, noting the exchange had lightened his mood. "Bring your guy over. Let me give my congratulations in person."

Nina's Don appeared properly dazzled by his fiancée and Knox chatted with the pair between filling drink orders. But soon they were gone and the revelry wound down. After the last customers left, Knox sent the staff home including Eban, offering to handle the final closing tasks on his own. "I have my own set of keys."

"We each have a set," Eban said, "thanks to you." He slapped Knox on the back. "I can't thank you enough for another great year, partner."

"*Silent* partner," Knox reminded him.

"We're still keeping it secret even though your dad—"

"Go home, Eban," Knox interrupted, unwilling to continue that conversation.

After a moment, the other man waved in acknowledgment and exited through the rear door.

In the new quiet, Knox noted he felt just as alone as he had when surrounded by a boisterous crowd.

His hand went to his pocket where he found the key that would bring him to some legacy he'd been left by his father. Aunt Claire had delivered it to him the night he'd met with his brothers in the bar. During the months that followed, worrying the piece of metal had become a habit—as had deliberately postponing a visit to the address that accompanied it.

Something ghostly brushed his arm and he started, only to see the stupid YOLO! balloon drift past him again, then finally surrender to gravity and fall to the confetti-and-ribbon strewn floor. Still clutching the key, he stared at it.

What the hell is wrong with me?
And what am I going to do about it?

On New Year's Day, despite a spare few hours of sleep, Knox joined the dawn patrol—what surfers called their sojourns in the water at sunrise. He drove north past Ventura and stopped south of Santa Barbara at a famous spot known around the world. Surfers were never alone at Rincon, even if the waves were onshore slop or the water smooth as glass. Today the swells were so-so and the sheer number of surfers enough to get him out after a shorter-than-usual session.

Still, he felt invigorated by the cold water, the strenuous activity, and even doing the rock dance— what was required to get into and out of the ocean on that stretch of coastline. It worked up an appetite too, so he stopped his Jeep at his favorite nearby taco stand to get the best start to the morning a man could ask for, a California burrito.

In the parking lot, with the sun streaming through his windshield and his driver's side window open to catch the ocean air, he munched on the huge flour tortilla filled with carne asada, cheese, guacamole, sour cream, salsa, and crispy French fries. The combined flavors on his tongue took him back to happy times—kicking back after a day on the sand, taking a break from a long ride on his motorcycle, at the 19th hole with his buddies following one of their crazy Worst Ball golf games.

Where was that carefree, fun-loving side of him?

A knock on the roof had him looking over and up. "Steamer," he said, grinning. "Steamer," after the famous surfing location in Santa Cruz, Steamer Lane, and the name everyone called this guy with his bleached dreads and the shell-and-leather cord necklace. The only other things he wore was a wetsuit and a pair of flip flops that looked to have been nibbled by fish around the edges.

"'Sup?" Steamer said. "Haven't seen you around."

"Yeah," Knox agreed. "But I had a hankering." He lifted the burrito.

"It'll cure just about anything," Steamer said. "I'm thinking of carne asada fries myself."

"Those'll do it too." Knox knew he was still smiling and was damn glad about it. "You take care."

"Will do." The surfer turned toward the taco stand, then turned back. "Hey, man," he said. "Sorry to hear about your dad."

And like that, Knox's dreary mood was back.

It hung over him like a dark cloud through his drive home, his shower, and up until he saw a familiar name on his cell phone screen.

He snatched up the device. "Max!" Fourth oldest Brannigan, former Navy SEAL, current protector of military contractors.

"How the hell are you, dude?" Knox added the "dude" because his brother always seemed to expect some surf lingo from him.

"Getting along," Max said.

"Still in a war zone?"

Not surprising, his brother ignored the last question. He always held the details of his work situation close to his—bulletproof—vest. "I had a moment to call. You doing okay?"

Knox could hedge too. "What makes you ask?"

"Just a feeling. Haven't heard from you in a while."

"You're the one who ignores the Brannigan email chain."

"We have a Brannigan email chain?" Max asked. "Are we also taking lessons in how to braid each other's hair?"

Knox had to laugh, and did that feel good. "You gotta admit you've been more out of touch than usual."

"Yeah." His brother's sigh sounded weary. "Been dealing with some shit."

"Shit—"

"Been dealing," Max said shortly, and it was clear that was all he would say.

Knox released his own sigh. If a Brannigan wasn't going to talk, he wasn't going to talk.

"Gabe says Dad's death is hitting you hard," his brother continued. "I heard you've been moping around."

"Gabe said that?" Knox demanded. This…thing he'd been grappling with lately wasn't about Colin, damn it. It was just some weird mood. "I've never moped a day in my life!"

"Exactly. So what's the deal? Aunt Claire told me she met a nice woman in her art class she thought you'd like and you wouldn't even take the number."

"Dude. You called from the other side of the world to tell me you think I should use Aunt Claire's matchmaking services?"

"I'm calling from the other side of the world, *dude*, because you're our ladies'-man, our bro who keeps the smiles coming, the Brannigan who's a fun junkie rather than the adrenaline kind. Not taking a pretty woman's number just doesn't sound like you."

Knox hesitated, then realized his free hand had slid into his pocket to find that infernal key once again. "I don't much feel like me," he finally admitted. His fingers clamped around the metal. "I'm stuck in a not-me rut."

"I heard from Luke too," Max said. "You haven't yet looked into the legacy Dad left you?"

"It's a key. And not one to a summer camp like Luke received or the family ranch like Gabe. The address that came with it is a storage unit. I looked it up." And what would Colin Brannigan have stored there for his second-youngest son? He was sure he'd been as much a cypher to his father as the man had been to him. Or maybe not...

You never take anything seriously!

"It's probably a clown suit," he muttered.

"Or maybe that live bunny you always begged for at Easter every year," Max said. "What if he left it there without four months' worth of food and water?"

Surely Colin wouldn't have bequeathed Knox a live gift—

"Screw you, Max," he said, as the other man's snicker traveled through the phone.

"Come on, admit I had you going for a second."

Knox shook his head, then withdrew the key from his pocket. It lay flat in his palm and he stared at it, wondering if the innocuous item was to blame for weighing him down. "Actually," he said slowly, "you do have me going." Was today really the day?

Yeah, he decided. It was action. Perhaps a way out of the rut. He'd been carrying the damn key around for weeks and weeks and it was time to put it to use. After all, it was a new year.

"What's that mean, Knox?"

"Open the next email I send, would you? It will tell you exactly what dear old Dad left behind for me."

Thirty minutes later, at a twenty-four-hour, air-conditioned storage facility located not far from his bungalow in Santa Monica, Knox blinked at the first sight of his legacy then let out a startled laugh.

While the bulk of Colin Brannigan's estate was to be distributed in five years, he'd left each of his sons something "personal." Brother Gabe had been given the family ranch in Calabasas, Luke the summer resort where Colin had met their mother. Hunter had been handed down a treasure map, of all crazy things. But who knew their dad owned a motorcycle?

Colin was a luxury cars and limousines kind of man. For kicks he might take a cruise on his yacht or a jaunt on his private jet with like-minded people of wealth and—purported—worth. Not in a million years could Knox picture his dad in boots and leathers, messing up his precisely styled haircut with a motorcycle helmet.

And this wasn't just any motorcycle. This pristine specimen was none other than a 1953 Indian Chief, one of only 600 produced, if Knox's memory served. He reached out a hand to caress the supple black leather seat.

"What the hell, Dad?" Knox would bet his last dollar that it was original from its chrome handlebars to its swooping rear fender. "Where did you find this bad-ass ride? And what did you mean by giving it to me?"

Though neither his father's ghost nor the storage unit walls answered, the very existence of the bike pointed in a single direction.

The open road.

Maybe there Knox would drop this persistent gloom and find his pleasure-seeking, live-for-the-moment, fun-and-games-and-grins-all-around true self again.

Chapter 2

—➔➤➤◄◄◄—

Mimicking the gesture of her two BFFs, Erin Cassidy lifted her margarita glass, the Moonstone Café logo facing front and center. "To...?" she questioned.

"To the Yoga Girl Studio, of course," redheaded Deanne said, "on the occasion of its second birthday!"

"And to our very own yoga girl," Marissa added, brushing back her blonde bangs with her free hand, "on the occasion of her 27th birthday."

"I'll drink to that." Erin clinked glasses with her friends then sipped at her salty-sweet beverage, shifting her gaze to take in the view over the railing of the café's beachside deck. "We even have the perfect Cinnabar, California sunset adding to the atmosphere."

"Only the best for you," Marissa said, grinning. "I put in my order for it weeks ago."

Erin released a little sigh of satisfaction. Yes, her

business had a birthday today, the yoga studio a modest success after two years of hard work. Small-town Cinnabar could have proved a challenge when it came to filling up classes, but thanks to the booming tourism industry in this part of California's central coast as well as her diligent efforts to reach out to the two nearby luxury resorts—one including a high-end spa—and the many B & Bs, drop-in visitors regularly added to her core local clientele.

She turned her gaze back to her friends, beaming at them. They'd been besties since third grade when Marissa moved to town. They'd gone through everything together including two weddings. Deanne and Marissa had married CPA brothers Rob and Tom Farmer, and Marissa was not quite eight months pregnant with her first child.

Erin narrowed her eyes and sent a pointed glance at her friend's glass. "Virgin margarita, right?"

"Of course." Then Marissa exchanged looks with Deanne. "Speaking of virgins…"

A niggle of caution worked its way down Erin's back, beneath the clingy black T-shirt she wore with a floral skirt and her sling-back black heels. "I thought we had that conversation-slash-confession when we were nineteen."

"They say it can't grow back, but I wouldn't be so sure," Deanne said, darkly. "Erin, here's the thing. We've discussed it and have decided you need to get out of the studio, babe, and find yourself a stud."

"Studio, stud." Marissa sent the redhead an admiring look. "I see what you did there."

Deanne fluffed the bottom of her hair. "I'm more than just a pretty face."

"That you are," Erin said, grasping for a quick

change of topic. "It's why you're doing so well at the title company. How's that new department head working out?"

Her friends pinned her with both their gazes. "Do we look that easy to distract?" Deanne demanded.

Erin swallowed. "C'mon—"

"Don't we always take the opportunity on our birthdays to reflect and correct?" Marissa pointed a finger at each of the other two at the table. "My 24th. You held an intervention about the blue and green streaks I was then sporting in my hair."

"They clashed with that traditional wedding dress you'd chosen," Erin reminded her. "And your mother-in-law was going around whispering she was planning to cut them out in your sleep."

"She's very scary when it comes to hairstyles." Marissa leaned forward, whispered, "It was a good call."

"See, Erin? You should listen to us." Deanne nodded for emphasis. "It's time to put yourself out there. Open up. *Loosen* up."

"I don't know what you mean," Erin mumbled.

Her friends rolled their eyes. "You're much too tightly wrapped. So disciplined—"

"That's the whole point of yoga! It's a discipline. A spiritual, mental, and physical practice—"

"You're using it to control your heart," Deanne said. "For a while, it made sense to us. You were smarting over that stupid guy. Then you were occupied with building your business. But Yoga Girl is going great and now it's time for *the* yoga girl to have a little fun again."

Anxiety constricted Erin's throat and she tried easing it with a swallow from her glass. "I've been out of the dating scene, sure. And maybe I'll take your advice and...and start thinking about re-entry, um, soon." Though the whole idea made her want to squirm. Allowing someone into her life who could ultimately hurt her, humiliate her... Bleh. Her heart had been deeply wounded once before when she'd thrown herself into what she'd believed was a mutual grand passion.

Better to be strong in body than soft of heart.

"Erin." Marissa reached for her hand, squeezed it. "You don't want to be ninety and supple but all alone."

"Oh, forget the future," Deanne said with a wave of her hand. "Start smaller. Think about the now. Let some man have the benefit of all your amazing flexibility."

That startled a laugh from Erin. "So you're just talking about sex."

"Nothing wrong with it." Deanne drained her glass then pushed it toward Erin. "Yes it's your birthday and yes, I gave them my credit card to cover the tab, but I think *you* should go to the bar for refills."

Erin frowned. "I can signal the server—"

"You need to look around, silly!" Marissa said. "Take a walk-through and see if there's anyone in the café who catches your eye."

"Wait. *Now?*"

"You're dressed up," Deanna said. "You're wearing make-up. You're sliding into old-maidhood faster than the rate Marissa's ankles are swelling into cantaloupes."

Instead of protesting the insult, her other friend slid her glass toward Erin too. They both had that steely look in their gazes that promised no surrender. So, on a sigh, she gave in.

"Fine," she muttered, gathering up the margarita glasses.

Next she threaded through the umbrella-topped tables on the deck. They were nearly full, customers in for a happy hour or an early dinner. She waved at one elderly couple she recognized who regularly took one of her morning classes.

Wide glass doors were thrown open from the deck that led to inside seating. Here, it wasn't hard to spot the spa tourists with their relaxed expressions, pampered skin, and new manicures all around. Seeing one studying a flyer from Yoga Girl—they were stocked in a rack near the entrance to the café along with other promotional material from local businesses—a spurt of gratification coursed through Erin's veins.

The feeling made her reckless enough to accept the freebie birthday tequila shot offered to her by the bartender, Adam, who was making the drinks she'd ordered. The liquor gave her a giddy jolt and she had to concentrate carefully to bring the fresh margaritas back to the table without spilling a drop.

Thirsty work. Upon seating herself, she downed a third of her new icy concoction.

"Well?" Deanne asked as she swallowed. Both she and Marissa were looking at her expectantly.

She set down her glass. "Well, what?"

Deanne frowned. "Did you see any likely candidates on your trip to the bar and back?"

"Oh." She cleared her throat. "I guess not."

"You didn't even look," Deanne said, throwing up her hands. "The situation is just that bad."

"Or maybe none of the men in this place are just that good." Erin took another swallow of margarita. "This isn't exactly the singles hot zone, you know."

"But you have to start noticing. Surveying. Opening yourself to possibilities." Deanne craned her neck to peer over Erin's shoulder. "And I spy a very interesting prospect just now seating himself at the bar."

On a sigh, Erin turned her head in time to see a man's back as he slid onto a stool . His thick black hair was disheveled, and he wore a beat-up black leather jacket, dark jeans, and a pair of lace-up motorcycle boots. Her belly clutched and her mouth went dry as her danger-dar went on full alert.

Bad boy! it shouted.

She'd learned to steer clear of that type six years before. A little too late, perhaps, but the lesson had stuck.

"Why don't you go over and talk to him?" Deanne suggested. "From the looks of him, he's new in town."

Passing through. Temporary. Never gonna stay. Never gonna get tied down.

"You could offer him tips about the local sights. That kind of thing."

"Truly? You think I should go hit on some stranger?" Erin tossed back the rest of her margarita and tried imagining it. Nope, not her style.

"For *practice*," Marissa said. "We're here, we have your back, so it wouldn't hurt to chat up a good-looking man."

Sexy man, Erin amended, taking another peek at him. With those wide shoulders and lean hips and that dangerous aura that came wrapped in black leather.

She swallowed. "Sorry, no. The first time you think of climbing back onto two wheels, you start with something much tamer than that."

Dismissing the idea altogether, she focused on Marissa and her almost eight-month-along pregnancy. "Let's talk about baby names. Any new ones to consider?"

To her astonishment, the pretty blonde burst into tears.

Erin's stomach dropped to her toes. "What is it? What's wrong? Are you hurting somewhere?"

Her friend frantically shook her head and reached for her purse to dig out tissues.

At a loss and barely holding back her panic, Erin looked toward Deanne. "Should we call Tom? The doctor?"

"No, no." Marissa mopped at her face. "I'm f-fine. R-really."

"What it is?" Deanne touched her sister-in-law's arm. "Tom will come immediately. You know he will."

"Why? I'm a cow. He married a cow."

Erin and Deanne exchanged another worried glance. "He wouldn't say such a thing," Erin said.

"And I'll have Rob kill him if he did," Deanne added. "Or take it back, Erin and I will do the deed ourselves."

Marissa released a watery laugh. "Thanks. He didn't actually say it, though. He didn't have to. I see it in the mirror."

"Honey—"

The mother-to-be gestured toward her body. "My boobs are huge and my belly ginormous and the button sticks out like a...like a button!"

Erin pressed her lips together to hide her amusement. Still, she felt for her friend. She'd had enough pregnant women in her yoga classes to know there came a time when their patience with the process began to wear thin. "Poor Rissa."

"You know what?" She poked at the offending little lump protruding through her stretchy maternity dress right in the middle of the baby bulge. "I wish this were an eject button. I am so ready to have this kid right this minute."

Then she turned feral eyes on Erin. "That's why *you* have to do it."

The wild gaze frightened her a little. "Have your baby? Uh, can't do that, pal."

"Then you have to distract me," Marissa said, in a low tone that meant business. "If I have to feel fat and drink virgin slushies and not have sex because Tom's afraid for the baby, then you have to walk over there and start something with that hot guy."

"Um, maybe you should take this up with Tom."

Alarm puckered her friend's pretty face. "I don't want Tom to talk to the hot guy! With a wife who looks like this and a man who looks like that, he might leave me for the other team!"

"Settle down." Erin glanced around the deck, worried they were attracting undue attention. "And really, we don't know what that guy actually looks like. I only see, um, leather." Jacket, motorcycle boots. Then those sinful tight jeans, too.

Danger.

Marissa made a shooing motion with her hands. "Well, go check it out!"

Erin appealed to Deanne. "You don't really expect me to 'start something' do you?"

"Just exchange a few words." Her gaze slid toward Marissa, and a worry line formed between her brows. "It would really do this one some good, I think."

Marissa's fingers spread over the bulge of her belly, and more tears sprang to her eyes. "*Moo*," she said, piteously. "*Moooo*."

On a sigh, Erin stood up. She wobbled a little, the tequila having shot straight to her head. "This is nuts. You're nuts."

Her pregnant friend swiped at another falling tear. "If it's a girl, we're considering 'Erin' for a middle name."

That did it. Hauling in a long breath, she turned, then set her sights on a pair of broad shoulders in battered black leather. She took a step toward him. Another.

Her fingers flexed as she imagined the pliant smoothness of that leather beneath the palms of her hands. She saw herself coming up behind him, sliding her arms around him to find his chest, nuzzling that glossy, messy hair of his with her mouth and breathing in the scent of hot, ready man.

Wait! Her feet stuttered to a stop. Where had that fantasy come from?

She glanced back at her BFFs. Deanne mouthed, "Go." Marissa plied the damp tissue again.

Feeling self-conscious and slightly tipsy and about fifteen instead of twenty-seven, Erin forced herself to continue. Then she was standing behind the stranger, her heart racing.

"Um…"

She saw his body go alert. His head turned slightly to the side.

Her mouth went dry. The profile looked as fine as the rest of him. "I... I..." She swallowed, desperate to think of something to say. "You, um, look kind of familiar. Did...did we have a class together?"

Now he swung all the way around, and she had to hastily step back to avoid his long legs and a topple into his lap.

She stared at him, his hair falling over his brow, the midnight eyes framed by dark lashes, the facial bone structure that turned angles and planes into pure masculine art. His mouth curved up to reveal a devastating, devilish smile. Her pulse throbbed at her wrists and at the vulnerable side of her neck. The air crackled.

Danger, her instincts warned again. *Danger*.

"What did you say, hon?"

She tried out her own smile and then repeated herself, because her brain couldn't come up with anything else. "Did we have a class together?"

Under his dark, intense gaze, all the tiny hairs on her body lifted and the air snapped again with electric intensity. That smile of his turned into a grin.

"Maybe so, darlin', because we sure have some chemistry."

She blinked, unsure. "Is that...is that..."

"It's a classic pick-up line." He patted the empty stool beside his. "Get comfortable, darlin', and we can have a conversation about it."

The brunette beauty sort of collapsed onto the seat next to Knox. "This is so embarrassing," she said, putting a slender hand over her eyes and shaking her head so that her sleek hair swirled around her shoulders. "I didn't know that was a pick-up line."

He shrugged. "I've heard much worse. I've probably used much worse."

"But I didn't mean for it to sound that way," she insisted.

"Uh-huh." He was regretting the impulse to invite her to sit down. It was something the old Knox would do automatically, but even a couple hundred miles on the Indian hadn't distanced him from the Knox of the low mood. That guy had merely climbed on the back of the bike to ride tandem, damn it all.

"I wasn't trying to pick you up, honest. Just chat you up." She groaned. "That doesn't sound any better, does it?"

"Don't give it another thought." Instead of looking at her, he focused on his beer. He'd planned a quick break and then back onto the bike to find a place to stop for the night up the coast. He'd have to remember, though, that he couldn't be too choosy. There was some empty road ahead.

Maybe he could ask the brunette for a suggestion—but no. No reason to prolong the encounter. He wasn't good company at the moment.

"It's the pregnancy," she suddenly said.

He shot her a quick glance. "You have a baby on the way?"

"Oh, not me." She put her hand over her flat belly, and he noted her skirt had hiked up above her knees to reveal inches of smooth thigh. She crossed one toned leg over the other. "One of my best friends. She's turned into a crier."

Looking away again, he brought his beer to his mouth. Politeness suggested he should offer to buy her a drink, but thank God that became a moot point when the bartender paused to take her order, and she said two margaritas and that shot of tequila she'd downed were enough—even on her birthday.

A tipsy birthday girl, Knox realized. Huh. There were country songs written about just this. Rom-com screenplays.

Hell, limericks on bathroom walls. The old Knox wouldn't have taken advantage of the situation, but he wouldn't have hesitated to flirt a little either. This Knox just wanted to be by himself.

"Your lips look lonely," he heard himself say anyway, and supposed some habits were so ingrained nothing could suppress them. "Would they like to meet mine?"

A quick laugh burst from the brunette. "What?"

"Another classic opener."

"Oh."

He glanced over, noting the curve of her full mouth. "Should I call you Google? Because you have every single thing I'm looking for."

"Hah." She laughed again. "A modern classic."

"As well as an in-the-moment question. What's your name?" Instinct was taking over again. Of course you always introduced yourself to a pretty girl. "I'm Knox Brannigan."

"I…" She hesitated, then shifted to face him as she held out her hand. "I'm Erin Cassidy."

"An Irish lass," he murmured in a terrible brogue. Then he shifted too, for the first time fully facing her as he clasped her fingers in his.

Starlight, he thought, dazzled, as he looked into the pale silver of her irises. And heat. So much heat. It shot up his wrist to his bicep to cuddle in his armpit before arrowing down his belly where it shocked his cock into sudden alertness. He grabbed for the bar with his free hand as the legs of his stool seemed strangely unsteady.

In his ears, he heard his quick indrawn breath and saw her do the same as the magnificent eyes staring into his widened.

What the hell is this?

But before he could decide, she backed off, her fingers sliding against his to free herself of his hold.

"Okay," she said, her expression confused. She called down the bar to the man behind it. "Hey, Adam. Another margarita after all, okay?"

Yeah. Knox needed to cool down as well. Raising a finger, he signaled for another round for himself. "Put hers on my tab," he murmured when the bartender came back with the drinks.

"Oh, no—" Erin began.

"Please." Then he ordered a few items from the appetizer menu. It wouldn't do to get drunk, not when he already had experienced that weird moment of vertigo. So weird, he ensured his arm stayed clear of hers as he passed her some of the stack of napkins Adam set before him.

She had her neck craned over her shoulder.

"What are you looking at?" he asked, glancing in that direction.

"My nutty friends. The ones who put me up to the bad pick-up line."

"'I seem to have lost my phone number, can I have yours?' is a bad pick-up line." He watched a platter of bruschetta and another of fried calamari slide between them and rubbed at the residual burn on his arm, still prickling after their brief contact. "And I thought you weren't trying to come on to me."

"They're both flashing me a thumbs-up sign," she

said, and groaned. "Can I turn in friends of almost twenty years for a different pair?"

When he looked this time, he identified her buddies by their avid scrutiny. Two pretty women, one obviously pregnant. "Wow. I hope you have the hospital on speed-dial for the mom-to-be in the blue dress."

"She has weeks to go yet. But that whole pregnant thing is the cause of our meeting like this. Marissa—the almost mom—feels the need for a distraction, and she and Deanne decided me inspecting the café for fresh meat would do the trick."

"Fresh meat." He kept his face straight. "It all sounds very romantic."

"They didn't use those words," she confessed. "It's only how I felt when I was instructed to approach. But she was tearing up, and there was something about maybe giving her baby my name in the middle which I really didn't buy, but what if they truly are considering it? Shouldn't I then try to give my best friend a pick-me-up by..."

"Picking me up?" he offered.

"Oh, God." She pressed her face into her hand for a silent moment. "I just replayed all that in my head. I can't imagine what you're thinking of me."

"You're a good friend. This is all no big deal." Except for that burst of heat when they touched. Those silver eyes, the color of the ocean right before dawn.

Letting her hand drop, she glanced over at him, her expression guilty. "For all I know you're married. I could have been trying to flirt with some other woman's husband."

"Not married. Don't imagine I ever will be—at

least I have no interest in the institution."

"Okay." She released a sigh. "Thank you for not being weirded out by this. Oh, and for not being a creeper."

"I try to keep that aspect of my character hidden until the second date."

A smile played at the corners of her mouth. "You're funny. And easy to talk to."

"Occupational hazard. Part-time bartender, so I spend a lot of hours speaking with people I don't know."

"What do you do with the rest of your time? When you're not making drinks and chatting with strangers?"

"This and that." Hardly anyone knew all the pies he put his fingers in. He'd not wanted to hear his father's judgment of his choices. "What about yourself?"

"Yoga instructor. I own a studio a few miles north of here. Well, it's actually my house, too, but I have a separate entrance and conduct classes on the bottom floor—" She broke off. "What? What's that look on your face mean? Why are you holding up your hand like a police officer halting traffic?"

"Yoga instructor," he said, sighing. "I need you to stop a second."

Her brows came together. "What? Why?"

"Give me just a minute." He closed his eyes. "I'm banishing all puerile and lascivious fantasies those two words bring to mind." Then his eyes popped back open. "Okay. I'm back. All clear."

She stared at him. "Um…have you ever taken a class?"

"*No.* And please don't bring up private lessons.

I'd have to go to a room by myself and think of goat shearing for an hour or two to tranquilize my overactive imagination."

"Goat shearing? That's a little creepy."

"Good to know." He nudged the bruschetta in her direction. "Hungry? I can't eat all this by myself."

When she hesitated, he smiled at her. "Hey, if I went too far with that shearing thing, you won't hurt my feelings if you head back to your friends." Maybe that would be for the best.

Instead of glancing their way, she delicately selected one of the bread rounds and slid it onto the small plate Adam had given her. "It's possible I'm having more fun with you. I know they'll be thrilled that I'm exchanging words with a man that are more than 'Salutation to the Sun' and 'Downward-Facing Dog.'"

He winced. "Erin…"

She batted innocent eyes. "Sorry, were those terms imagination-stimuli? Completely unintentional, I promise you."

"You're getting good at poking the fresh meat."

She laughed.

Then they both did as they ate and drank and swapped small talk, and Knox told himself that the warmth in his belly was beer and food and nothing more. He'd been half-buzzed in the company of an attractive woman many times, and this wasn't a new feeling. Right? But then her friends left and she didn't go with them because he was in the middle of telling her about his road trip. Not the nitty gritty, just that he'd obtained a new-to-him bike and decided to take some time off to drive up the coastal highway.

"Erin," he started. "You can leave—"

"It's fine." She put her hand over his where it rested on the bar. "Finish what you were saying."

He stared at their stacked fingers, every thought evaporating as her touch once again undid him— heating his skin, hardening every muscle, making his cock jump to attention once more. Without thinking, he turned his hand so they were palm-to-palm.

Damn.

Forcing his gaze up, he noted her eyes were fixed on the sight. Then she looked up, too.

"Hey," he said, softly, as a non-threatening acknowledgement of this potent force between them.

She swallowed, then replied in the same tone. "Hey."

But the shadow of worry in her eyes had his common sense reasserting itself, and he casually slipped his hand free to reach for his beer. This wasn't the time or place to start something, no matter how enticing the woman. "You know any bar tricks?"

From the corner of his eye, he saw her posture relax. "No, but something tells me you do."

"I'm all about fun and games."

Then he showed off a few of his pub cheats—the Snifter and the Cherry, the Toothpicks into Star, the Dime and Bottle. That one required a playing card that he pulled from the set stuffed into the pocket of his jacket. After he'd impressed her with the stunt, she snatched up the thin rectangle of plastic-coated cardboard.

"What's this?" she asked, inspecting the bright artwork.

"It comes from a strategy game some friends of mine developed. It took off Christmas before last and continues to prove popular. Maybe you've heard of it?

Greetings from an Admirer."

"I have! The goal is to deduce who your admirer is, right? But I've never played."

He put the entire pack in her hands. "Now you can."

"Right now?"

"Well, I do have one more trick to share."

"Show me."

Knox grinned at her eagerness. "You're storing up knowledge for the next time you're picking up fresh meat in a bar."

She made a face. "Just get on with it."

It didn't take long to explain how to get a dime out of an empty shot glass without touching it.

After going over the steps, he said, "You try it," and pushed the glass with the coin at the bottom in her direction.

Bending toward it, she hesitated. "Like this?" Her silver eyes slid to him.

"Yeah." His scalp began tingling as his attention shifted to her mouth. "You know. It's simple. Put your lips together and…blow."

She stilled for a moment, but then she puffed, the dime popped out, and he thought he might just lose his mind when she straightened, her face flushed in triumph, her lips still in kiss-position.

Their gazes met, and then her hands began fanning her cheeks. "Kind of hot in here."

"Yeah." He hauled in a breath. "Kind of hot. Maybe we should go outside. Get some air."

She swallowed. "Actually, I should probably head home. The café closes at nine, and…"

"Yeah." He glanced around, noticing the tables had mostly cleared out and only a couple of the staff remained. So their interlude was over. "I'll walk you to your car."

The outside air was chilled and smelled of saltwater and stars. The beach was a half-block away, and he could hear the surf and the click of Erin's heels on the blacktop. She rubbed her bare arms as they walked and he immediately shrugged out of his jacket to drape it over her shoulders.

"It's only a few feet," she said.

He shushed her protest, then stood while she dug through her purse for the key fob to her boxy little car. "Cute," he commented lightly. "Like you."

Her head lifted as she drew out the small device. "Well, Knox Brannigan, I guess this is goodbye." She moved to pull off the coat, but he stopped her by gripping a zippered edge in each hand.

"Not quite yet," he murmured, and used his hold to draw her closer.

Angling his head, he brushed her mouth with his. She quivered within the leather of his coat, but her mouth was warm, and she didn't protest or pull away.

"Yeah, darlin'," he murmured against her lips and then pressed harder so that she opened and his tongue could take a foray inside.

Heat. Wet. Sweet.

He fisted the leather to stop his greedy hands from running over her body, but the taste of her kiss tempted him, goaded him, shoved him toward something he'd never known before.

Her tongue slid along his, and his belly tightened. His hips jerked and his cock pressed against her belly. Erin gasped and stepped back.

Idiot, he told himself. Retreating too, Knox lifted his hands. "Sorry. I got carried away."

"No. It was me too. I also got carried away." She slid his jacket from her shoulders and held it out. "Thank you. Thank you for everything. Your friendliness, the bar tricks, the card game."

With a nod, he watched her get into the car. Slipping his arms through the sleeves of his jacket he detected a lingering trace of her perfume.

Her car door shut, he heard the click of the locks, then the engine turned over. As she began to reverse, her window rolled down. She smiled at him, like she had when she first sat down, a little shy. Very, very sweet.

"And thanks for the kiss," she said, and motored away.

As he watched her tail lights recede, Knox couldn't shake the unwelcome feeling that in a season of loss, he'd just suffered another.

Chapter 3

Morning was pitch-black when Erin's alarm went off, set so she'd get up in time to lead her Sunrise Seniors class. She went through her usual motions—made the bed, showered, brewed a pot of green tea, letting it steep as she dressed. All the while she refused to dwell on the events of the night before.

And her companion.

It was much more sensible to forget the shape of Knox's face, his muscled height, the brightness of his smile. His easy manner—forget it. Everything about him, she told herself, was too easy.

Too experienced, too smooth. Like Teflon, he was the kind of man who wouldn't stick.

Didn't she know that type?

She'd sworn off them six years before, sitting in a crappy motel room with an empty wallet and an equally empty tank of gas.

"Don't think about that either," she muttered to

herself as she opened drawers.

She dug two layers down to find her favorite yoga outfit. Blue cropped leggings with mesh panels up the the side; a blue-black-and-white strappy bra over which she wore an open-back tank that knotted at the small of her back. She slipped on the matching hoodie as she returned to her tiled kitchen to pour tea into the mug sitting on the counter by her phone.

Which showed the recent arrival of a text. From Marissa. *Call me.*

Erin didn't hesitate. "What's the matter? Are you feeling okay?" she asked when her friend picked up. "Why are you awake so early?"

"Because baby is up and kicking and my bladder is the size of a walnut. I wanted to catch you before your first class."

"Oh. Well." Her concern vanquished, Erin sipped from her mug. "Thanks again for yesterday evening."

"Oh. My. God." Marissa's voice rose two octaves. "Does that mean what I think it means? You took him home? Is he there now? Was it the best night ever?"

Erin rolled her eyes. Her pregnant friend often saw life as a series of schmaltzy cable movies. Likely she was envisioning that Erin had experienced a romantic adventure that could be titled along the lines of "Romancing the Margarita."

"Well?" Marissa prompted.

"He's not here now."

"Oh." Marissa sighed. "Then at least tell me about the sex. Give me all the details because you know these days I can only live vicariously when it comes to that."

"I didn't even bring him home." Erin shook her

head. "Really, Rissa. Your imagination is working overtime."

Her friend's mood seemed to deflate on another sigh. "This could be true."

"Though I have it on good authority that contemplating goat shearing can help control that," she added, and felt herself smile.

"Huh?"

Erin quickly wiped it away. "Never mind."

"So nothing happened? Really?"

"Before the café even closed we said our goodbyes and went our separate ways. Nothing happened." Just electric touches that had made her hyper-aware of every cell and every sensation. Yoga practice encouraged being mindful of one's body, and she'd never been so mindful as when she was seated beside Knox. She'd been aware of the blood wooshing through her veins, the shallow breaths that couldn't seem to find the bottom of her lungs, the tight stretch of every nerve.

The kiss had left her mouth feeling like a pincushion—swollen and tingling with tiny, delicious pricks.

He was the most delicious man she'd ever met.

But she was forgetting him. Right. This. Instant.

"Did he smell good? I really love a good-smelling man."

Though she didn't want to stay on this topic, it was hard to ignore the plaintive tone in Marissa's voice. "Honey, shall I pick up some new aftershave for Tom today?"

"I don't want new aftershave for Tom," her friend said, her tone turning strident. "I want to know what that stranger smells like."

Yeesh. Pregnancy could make a woman's moods erratic. "All right, all right."

"Well?"

"Knox—"

"His name is Knox? That sounds so cool."

"His name is Knox," Erin confirmed. "I should have introduced you."

"We didn't want to interrupt. The two of you looked so…engaged." Marissa lowered her voice. "Tom's up now, but I won't get off the phone until you describe the way this cool Knox smells."

Erin shook her head, but tried to find the right words. "He smells like…like good leather and fresh air and…" What else? A pheromone specifically designed to get past Erin's guard? Because she'd dropped it enough to actually flirt with the man. That mention of Downward-Facing Dog had been no accident.

Which reminded her… She checked the clock.

"Look, Rissa. I have to go this second and open up the studio or I'll be late for my first class."

"Okay." Marissa sighed. "I only want to know one more thing. Any regrets that you let him get away? You looked as if you were really into him."

Erin *had* been really into him. But he was a guy passing through. "None whatsoever," she said in a firm voice. "It was a chance encounter. A page now turned. He's officially banished from the planet of my thoughts forever."

Famous last words, she discovered, because twenty minutes later the man in black leather walked into her studio, and in the soft early-morning light he looked more dangerous—and more delicious—than ever.

Panic sweat instantly trickled down her spine.

Most of the class had already arrived and were arranging their mats in their usual order—once a person established a position in the room they seemed to stick to it. Gertie and Jean and Carol were still chatting near the entrance, however, dressed in pastel leggings and tunics and holding matching water bottles. Turning as one, they went silent to stare at Knox as he glanced around the room, his gaze honing in on Erin.

Her entire body tensed as their eyes met and her stomach jittered.

What is he doing here?

Aware of the curious onlookers, she threaded through the mats to come to stand a few feet from him. His hair was more disheveled than the previous night, and there was a dark shadow of whiskers on his jaw and around his mouth.

She couldn't look away from it.

That kiss. There'd never been another one like it. Tender then bold. His tongue sliding against hers with such confidence that she'd wanted to open her mouth wider for him, melt against his body, offer him everything.

"I found this vagrant hanging around outside." An older male's voice broke through her reverie.

Her gaze jumped to gray-haired and grumpy Earl Baker, who accompanied his wife to yoga, griping about it all the while until his back pain eased by the end of the fifty minutes.

"He doesn't look like a vagrant to me," Carol piped up, an appreciative gleam in her eye.

"Then why was he hanging around the entrance? He's not gonna take yoga in denim pants and a leather jacket." Earl sent the younger man a hard look.

"He's not a vagrant." Erin shifted her gaze to Knox. "What's going on?"

"He's a hobo then," Earl said. "Riding the trains that come through town."

"Earl, he's not a hobo," Erin replied, holding back her exasperation.

"Not dressed for yoga," Earl pointed out again.

"That's true," Knox said, speaking for the first time. He aimed a half-sheepish smile at the women gathering closer. "Sorry to barge into your class, ladies."

Erin ignored the growing audience. "But what are you doing here?"

"It's a long story."

Earl settled his arms across his chest. "We have nowhere to be. Retired, all of us. Well, except Erin."

Now she looked around at her interested students. "Why don't you all get settled on your mats while I handle this? It shouldn't take more than a couple of minutes."

With a few murmurs and another dark look from Earl, they shuffled off, giving her and Knox some space. Still, she moved closer for additional privacy, close enough that she smelled the leather of his jacket. He looked down at her, his dark eyes fixed on her face, a bemused half-smile on his mouth, his mood a complete mystery to her.

She swallowed. "Knox, what are you doing here?"

He hesitated.

Erin's stomach jittered again, and her breath caught in her throat as she imagined what he might say.

I thought we made a special connection last night.

I couldn't leave after that amazing kiss.

His hand forked through his hair. "The thing is…"

I didn't sleep at all. I just had to come back and see you again.

She swallowed. "Yes?"

"My bike broke down."

"Oh." Though he couldn't know what she'd been thinking, her face flushed with embarrassment. He wasn't here because she'd been impossible to leave behind—a lesson she had already learned, right? "Your bike broke down."

"Yeah. Last night, after you left, I went for a long walk on the beach. The café was closed when I made it back to the parking lot, and I climbed on my bike, heading northward again. After a couple of miles the thing just refused to go farther."

"What did you do?"

"Cursed. Yanked out the owner's manual and started tinkering. Cursed some more. Eventually gave up and began walking."

"There's not much on that stretch of highway."

"I figured that out. I ended up sleeping on the beach until first light, then started walking again. When I saw your yoga studio, I decided to stop by." Shrugging, he shot her a small grin. "So, sort of like a vagrant."

"A phone call—"

From his inside coat pocket, he pulled out the semblance of a smartphone. "Unfortunately, I stepped on it in the dark while trying to figure out what was wrong with the bike."

"Oh," she said again.

He shoved the mangled device away and pulled something else from the back pocket of his jeans. The vehicle's owner's manual, it appeared. "See this?" His forefinger indicated a label pasted on the front cover. "It's north of here, I think. Not too far. Mickey's Motorcycle Sales & Repair. My bike, well, it's an exotic one and I was actually headed there to get the bike checked out by people possibly familiar with the machine. Now I'm hoping they can get it running again. Do you know the place?"

"Yes. It just so happens I do." She checked the clock on the wall. "Though it's too far to walk and no one will answer the phones for another hour."

Hesitating, she thought, *what to do?*

He'd been kind the night before.

That kiss.

Charming and funny.

That kiss.

Then there were the tricks he'd taught her, not to mention the gift of the card game.

That kiss!

Yes, that kiss. To prove she was over the inconsequential thing, that the page was definitely turned and maybe even pasted shut to boot, she was duty bound to make the offer, wasn't she?

"I'll take you there," she told Knox, ignoring instant misgivings. "As soon as yoga class is finished."

Then she marched to the front of the room, flipped on the music, and took her place.

At twenty-one years old, after she'd woken in the shoddy motel room to find herself alone and robbed of her money, her gas, and her self-respect, Erin had called her father and then waited for his arrival. Without a word of recrimination, he'd put fuel in her tank then followed her home. She'd spent the entire return journey calling herself all kinds of a fool.

A week later, Marissa had hauled her from a fetal position to a yoga class at the local rec center. Short minutes into that first class Erin was hooked. The teacher didn't stay in the area long—she too followed a man out of town, but Erin liked to believe he'd never abandoned her and they were happily deep breathing together somewhere.

The instructor had explained the connection between body, breath, and mind. Through conscious breathing and while moving through different poses, the practitioner created an inner harmony and removed herself from the chaos of the outside world to find a peace within.

Wonderful.

Then the instructor had said that through yoga one could be in the driver's seat of life.

She'd liked the sound of that even better.

And Knox Brannigan's unexpected arrival wasn't going to knock her out from behind the wheel. Later this morning they'd exchange a second round of goodbyes and it would mean nothing to her. Nothing but another dab of glue to keep that turned page forever closed.

Knox held a vague idea of what went on during a session of yoga. He'd been dragged to a spin class or two with this vegan he'd dated for a while. And sure, he'd stared through the plate glass window of the Pilates studio not far from The Wake and shook his head at the complicated machinery. But he was more of a surfing, running, and occasional free weights guy, so it was no surprise he was fascinated by the class's slow progression through stretches and poses.

Oh, fine. He was fascinated by the class's leader. The bright athletic wear molding her lithe figure allowed him to appreciate every taut muscle in her arms, legs, and torso. With her dark hair coiled in a dancer's bun on the top of her head, the pretty angle of her jaw and the slim line of her neck were revealed as well.

She moved like a dancer too, with grace and a lightness of body that immediately roused male instincts. Protection, to name one, he thought, watching the delicate curve of her fingers as she reached upward. And possession, as unearned as that might be. Then she rose from her mat to approach a student, and he found himself staring at her bare feet, with their high arches and shell pink-tipped toes. His skin blazed with heat.

Protection, possession, and lust.

A brightly lit room surrounded by senior citizens was no place for a man to lose control, so Knox shrugged out of his jacket and turned away from her. Staring out the nearby window, he watched the sun edge higher in the sky.

The night before, he'd never expected to see Erin again. Even when he'd been lying on the beach, under the thin emergency blanket he'd pulled from one of the bike's saddlebags, he'd refused to think of what might have been if she'd invited him home instead of driving off. He'd stacked his hands behind his head and stared upward, taking in the smudge of the Milky Way in the star-peppered sky.

And set his mind to thinking about why his father

had left him that particular gift. Why the vintage Indian?

The brothers before him who had dealt with their legacies had found value in them…value beyond any price tag. They'd discovered messages—though mostly unspoken—that their father left to them. It had given them a new peace with the man.

But Knox didn't know if any reconciliation—even one beyond the grave—could happen between him and Colin. He wasn't convinced his father wanted that with his second-youngest son, anyway. There'd been so much acrimony during those months he'd worked for the man. Afterward, a distant politeness existed between the two on the rare occasions they'd met. Neither of them had ever taken the initiative to hash out the old hurts.

Brannigan men weren't big on discussing their feelings.

So Colin's reason behind passing on the motorcycle remained an enigma. Recently Luke had said that their father hadn't liked to make things easy for his sons. Knox knew that to be true in his case since upon examination of the Indian the only "clue" he'd discovered was the address of the motorcycle shop. Without anything else to go on, that day in the storage unit he'd decided to head in its direction.

Last night, however, shivering behind a sand dune, he'd considered dropping the whole idea, reading the botched beginning as a bad portent. In the morning he'd call a tow truck or find a rental, load up the motorcycle and take his sorry ass back home.

Then, unbidden, Erin had popped into his mind. Her silver eyes and shy smile, her laughter and her light, addicting perfume. *I own a studio a few miles north of here.*

In that moment, it had seemed an incentive to continue on his journey. He didn't expect anything to come of visiting her, of course, but it had been enough last night to set his course. However inexplicable the urge, he'd wanted one more glimpse of her beautiful face.

"Knox?"

He jumped, looking over to see she stood at his elbow. "Yes?"

"Class is over. We'll leave in just a few minutes."

"Okay. Thanks." Shoving his arms back into his jacket, he noted the students were rolling their mats, tucking them under their arms, then heading for the exit.

Each stopped to say a few words to Erin.

Old man Earl paused to deliver a glare at Knox, pointing forked fingers at his own eyes then turning them on the younger man.

Biting back his grin. Knox tried looking properly cowed, then caught Erin watching the two of them. She shook her head.

"I see that, young lady," Earl addressed himself to the yoga teacher. "But mark my words, hobo or no hobo, this is a wild one."

"It's the leather jacket." A woman who had to be nearing eighty sidled close to stroke Knox's sleeve. "And the boots. Like Steve McQueen and Marlon Brando. *Those* were wild men."

Wearing a little smile, Erin shook her head again and then ushered the last of her students from the studio. "See you later."

Knox's elderly admirer turned and trained bright eyes on him. "Will *you* be here?"

"Just passing through," he said. "I'll be heading up the coast later today."

"And we'll get on that," Erin said briskly as she shut the door. "I won't be but a minute."

Only a few more than that and he folded himself into the passenger seat of her little car.

"I really appreciate the ride," he said, glancing over at her.

She'd put on a sweatshirt, and her face was still flushed from the exertion of teaching. A few tendrils had freed themselves from her bun to brush her temples and cheeks.

He didn't touch them.

He didn't take them between his fingers and thumb to caress their silky texture.

Though the curve of her ear tempted him, he didn't tuck those stray locks behind it.

He only imagined all that.

She reached for the travel mug between the seats. "You're sure you don't want some green tea? You could have this. It's fresh."

"I'm not really a green tea kind of guy," he said, as they pulled onto the highway. He gazed out the window. On one side the train tracks ran between the blacktop and the stretch of sand leading to the ocean. On the other, land stood empty except for scrub and grasses. Rolling hills loomed in the distance. The glare from the bright sun had him pulling on his sunglasses.

"It's going to be a beautiful winter day," Erin said.

"Looks like it."

She cleared her throat. "Too bad you had to sleep on the beach last night."

"I survived. And without the SoCal light pollution, the stars were incredible."

A bump in the road caused her Thermos of tea to rattle in the holder. "You knew I didn't live far…"

He glanced over to see her attention on the road, but a new flush of pink stained her face. "I wouldn't show up and scare you like that, Erin. Even if only to borrow your couch."

"Of course. Right." She nodded quickly.

"And I wouldn't have just wanted to borrow your couch."

Eyes wide, she looked over at him and then returned her attention forward. "Well."

The car hit another bump and her insulated cup popped up. They both reached for it, and their hands met. As it settled back in the holder, their fingers remained entwined.

Heat rocketed through him again. Lust, yes, but there was something else too. Caution? Concern? That need to protect her, he supposed, even if it was from himself.

But he didn't release her hand.

"This is…" Erin licked her lips. "Weird."

"Yeah." He brought their joined hands to his mouth and brushed his lips across her knuckles. "And new to me."

"Me as well."

He rubbed his jaw with the backs of her fingers. "But I don't suppose you do one night stands."

"No."

Not surprised, he let her go.

They went silent as she took the next exit that led to a small gathering of commercial businesses surrounded by humble stucco homes. They passed a gas station with attached convenience store, a grocery, a taco stand, and a pancakes-and-burgers place. Another half-block, and she turned in to a parking area with a neon sign that read *Mickey's* hovering above a two-bay garage connected to an office. A few motorcycles with For Sale signs hanging from the handlebars were parked out front. A house stood behind the repair business.

As she came to a halt, Erin hopped out of her car, and a big gray bear of a man strolled from one of the bays, dressed in coveralls and wiping his hands on a red shop rag.

Knox climbed from his seat as he watched Erin go on tiptoe to kiss the grizzled guy's whiskered cheek.

"How are you?" she asked him.

"Fine, fine." He air-patted her general vicinity, as if loathe to soil her bright clothes.

She stepped back and looked him over with a practiced eye. "Really? I heard from Jolly that your arthritis is flaring up again."

The man put his hands behind his back. "Jolly talks too much."

"Well, I'm coming back this afternoon to do your laundry for you."

"You don't have to—"

"And I'll bring my chili, too."

The old guy smiled. "Cornbread?"

She laughed. "And cornbread." On tiptoe again, she gave him another peck. "See you later."

Knox hadn't moved from his side of the car and now she hurried over to him. "Come on. Cass will help you with your motorcycle." She pointed. "That's Cass Cassidy, my dad."

Her dad. Huh. "Not Mickey?"

"His older brother. Gone now, but my father took over for Uncle Mickey a couple of years ago."

Damn. The date on the pink slip indicated Colin had owned the Indian much longer than that, meaning any information about his ownership of the bike had likely gone to the grave with Mickey Cassidy.

Erin nodded toward her father. "Tell him about your bike. I'm certain he can help you out."

"Sure. Okay." Knox hesitated, though, because Cass Cassidy was sending him a look so suspicious that it made Earl's glare seem like a virtual love letter. Telling himself the man couldn't know the dastardly and debauched designs Knox had spun around his daughter, he squared his shoulders. "Thanks."

"And goodbye," she said, her voice going soft. "I...well, I enjoyed meeting you. Happy trails and all that."

He caught her hand and stroked his thumb over the top, a brief, final caress. "Happy life, Erin."

"I'll be right here hoping for it." Then she slipped her fingers free and turned toward her father to wave as she tucked herself behind the steering wheel once more. "Bye, Dad! Take good care of this new customer."

Cass Cassidy lumbered closer, his bristly brows drawn together over narrowed, flinty eyes as he looked between his daughter and Knox. "A new customer? Who is this exactly?"

Before Knox could introduce himself, Erin sent him a blinding, mischievous smile that hit him right in the solar plexus. Then she cut her gaze back to her dad.

"Just some guy I picked up in a bar last night!"

she said, gunned the car, and was gone.

Knox sucked in a breath and turned toward the mechanic, noting his distrustful expression hadn't eased, and that a massive lug wrench hung from the loop of fabric at his hip. The tool could take a man out with one swing.

So he reached for his most charming smile but stayed outside of striking distance. "Nice to meet you. Sir."

Hours later he watched Erin's cute ride toodle into the parking area of the repair business. Leaning on the push broom he was wielding, he watched her climb out of her car, surprise on her face. "You're still here."

"Yeah." He couldn't tell if she was pleased or disappointed. "By the way, I owe you for that little stunt about being the man you picked up last night."

"Oh." Her expression turned sheepish. "Sorry. I like to tease Dad sometimes." She glanced around. "He nearby?"

"On the phone in his office."

Erin nodded at the broom. "And you're playing assistant?"

"Part of my plan to convince him not to kill me, cut me into little pieces, and throw me to his pack of vicious guard dogs."

"He doesn't have a pack of vicious guard dogs."

"Good to know. But that's not what he says."

"Really, though. Your bike?"

"We retrieved it, and he's been working on it." Not for the first time, Knox wished he knew his way around an engine like he knew his way around a cocktail menu or a business plan. "Cass has yet to deliver a complete diagnosis, but I have hopes I'll be on my way before dark."

"That's good."

"Yeah."

He watched her move to the rear of her car and pop open the hatchback. She half-bent to gather some canvas grocery bags. His gaze zeroed in on her ass.

His muscles drew tight, and the back of his neck burned. Her body...well, hell, it was nothing less than spectacular. She wore the same clinging outfit from the morning and he noted the mesh that marched up the side of the leggings, sheer enough that he could see a hint of skin beneath the long panel.

A hint of skin all the way from ankles to waist.

She couldn't be wearing anything underneath that stretchy fabric, right?

God, he wanted to take her somewhere private and quiet where he could bury his face in the skin of her neck as he peeled away those maddening clothes. His movements would be slow, careful, even though just thinking about it made his heart thrum and his breathing turn ragged.

Be cool, Brannigan.

She doesn't do one night stands, he reminded himself.

Even if you took a room in that motel down the road, she wouldn't join you there.

As she struggled to gather more bags, he broke from his lust-induced stupor and hurried forward. "Here," he said. "Let me get those for you."

Toe-to-toe with Erin, he made to scoop his arms beneath the canvas sacks. The back of his hands slid up her torso and brushed the outside of her breasts.

They both froze. Erin's gaze jumped to his, and

he lost himself in their silver depths. Under her clothes, he could feel her skin heating. She trembled and he wanted to kiss her, run his tongue along the edge of her jaw, take a bite of her small earlobe.

But he didn't move.

She doesn't do one night stands!

And that's all he had to give. Some fleeting passion, a little bit of carnal fun, and it was something he perversely both wanted to offer her and also shield her from.

Because Erin Cassidy deserved serious, promise-filled forevers. Precisely what he didn't have in him.

The office door screeched as Cass Cassidy threw it open. Erin leaped away from Knox, leaving him holding the bags and hoping like hell his stiff cock wasn't making itself known to her father.

The older man studied his daughter a long, silent moment, then he shifted his gaze. "Well, young Knox, bad news."

Knox knew it already. Erin Cassidy had bewitched him with her starry eyes and shy smiles. With her full mouth and her sleek curves. A spell that caused him to crave getting close while wanting to keep her distant at the very same time.

It didn't make sense. Knox had never set himself up as any woman's white knight. But he'd been off his game for weeks, and now he was beginning to worry he'd never be the same man again.

Erin threw Knox a nervous glance then cleared her throat. "What bad news is that, Dad?"

Cass turned to his daughter again. "The necessary part for the Indian has been difficult to track down. And I'd say it'll be at least three days before this young man will be ready to ride out of town."

Chapter 4

In the laundry room inside her father's small home, Erin pulled another towel from the basket and folded it with precise movements, then added it to the stack on the counter. Her friend Deanne had always hated doing laundry. Marissa merely put up with it. Now both had turned it into a joint husband-and-wife chore.

Though Erin had no spouse with whom to share the work, she didn't mind. In fact, she relished the simple task that resulted in stacks of fresh-smelling fabric and found it could calm her mind. Today included the added bonus that she was relieving her father of what he considered drudgery. His arthritic hands could really use the reprieve.

Plucking another still-warm length of terrycloth from the pile, she brought it to her nose, breathing in the clean scent. She closed her eyes and imagined a peaceful meadow, with clothes pinned to a line strung between two trees, the material swaying in a gentle breeze.

"Hey, there."

She jumped, serenity fleeing at the sound of Knox's voice. Clutching the cloth to her chest, she whirled toward the doorway.

He lingered there, wearing jeans, boots, and a navy waffle-weave Henley. "Sorry. I didn't mean to scare you."

"I'm not afraid," she said, frowning at him.

"Right." With his chin, he indicated a jumble of what looked to be more laundry that he held in his arms. "Your dad asked me to bring in these coveralls from the garage."

"Put them in that basket," she said, pointing.

He hesitated. "There's a towel and washcloth, too. Cass let me use the spare bathroom earlier today to take a shower."

"I know. I smelled your soap and shampoo." Erin cringed, hating how she'd given away her awareness of him. But the scent had been impossible to ignore as she traversed the hallway.

"I hope you don't mind."

She spared him a glance. "Why would I? This is my dad's home."

"Ah. You didn't grow up here?"

"When Uncle Mickey died, Dad moved in and left me the house where I am now."

"I see." He continued to linger.

Erin picked out a clean pillowcase and snapped it straight before folding. "It's too bad about the part for your bike," she said, glancing his way again. "I'm sorry for your inconvenience."

"Can't be helped."

She swallowed, then asked the question that had been at the forefront of her mind since her father had emerged from his office. "What will you do?"

"You mean...?"

She shrugged one shoulder.

"Well..." he said, drawling it out. "Cass did say you had an extra bedroom at your place."

Her hands jerked, an involuntary movement, which knocked one of the clean piles to the floor.

"Oh!" Face flaming, she bent to retrieve the scattered items. In her peripheral vision she spied the toes of his boots stepping up. "I can do it."

"I can help."

That clean fragrance of his was in her lungs now as they straightened, each holding some sheets and pillowcases. She snatched his share and arranged them into a new stack.

Knox touched her shoulder. "Erin."

Biting her lip, she turned to him.

"I was just joking around," he said.

"I knew that," she lied.

"Yeah?" He tilted his head, gazing into her face.

The expression on his—a warmth, a *tenderness*—made her feel shaky inside, unsettled. Nothing like her normal serene, disciplined self. One of his hands reached to tuck a strand of hair behind her ear, and the sensation of the pads of his fingers against the skin behind it made her nipples bud.

His voice lowered, nearly to a whisper. "Are you a magician? Because when I look at you everything else disappears."

A flush of heat broke over her flesh, and the tips of her breasts tightened more. "W-what?"

His arm dropped and, looking away, he cleared

his throat. "Just one of those cheesy pick-up lines I hear from behind the bar."

She should tell him to go away, she thought, trying to pull in a cleansing breath of air. There was no reason for him to be hanging around the repair business, let alone hanging around *her*.

"Knox—"

"I like your dad," he said.

Erin blinked. "Oh. Thanks."

He smiled. "Though I think he's still suspicious of me after your line about us meeting in a bar."

The easy grin soothed her some. "Probably not. He let you shower here after all." Her mind drifted away for a moment, thinking of that muscled body under the spray in the nearby shower, soap bubbles rolling down his pectoral muscles, his abs, over his—

"He reminded me of the dogs again before he let me inside his house."

The image burst—thank goodness—like one of the bubbles. "I told you," she said, half-exasperated. "He doesn't have any dogs."

"I don't know." He shook his head. "Maybe he keeps them chained up somewhere when you're around."

What a tease. But his grave demeanor gave nothing away.

Knox leaned his back against the folding counter and crossed his feet at the ankles. "Have any potential boyfriends reported similar threats?"

Surely he didn't consider himself "boyfriend" potential! But the notion—however ridiculous—that he might, settled under her heart, nudging it up toward her throat. "You're such a kidder."

"Just saying that your dad seems like the kind of

man who'd look very closely at guys hanging around you."

"There haven't been guys hanging around," she said shortly. Anything to put an end to the conversation and get him out of the laundry room, its dimensions seeming to shrink by the second. "No guys—like you mean—for a long time."

His brows jumped. "Odd," he murmured.

She wasn't "odd," she was careful. But Deanne's voice echoed in her head. *It's time to put yourself out there. Open up. Loosen up.*

Instead of looking at Knox, she applied herself to folding again, even as she was hyper-aware of his close regard. For a few minutes she ignored it, then she shot him a sidelong glance. "What? Do I have dryer lint in my hair or something?"

"Or something." And in a quick move, he yanked on the pony tail holder holding her coiled hair in a bun. The strands tumbled from the top of her head over her shoulders. Then he was combing through them with the fingers of one hand, as if he couldn't help himself. She froze, everything still but her scrambling pulse.

"Damn it, Erin," he said softly, though he sounded as if he was cursing himself. "Damn it all."

She wanted to turn into his touch. Press her face into his big hand, press her body against his tall one and take the strength and heat he offered.

It's time to put yourself out there. Open up. Loosen up.

But she couldn't seem to move. Thankfully. Or no.

Knox left off playing with her hair to move back to the entry. She risked a glance at him. He gripped the jamb on each side as if to anchor himself. "I booked a room at the motel down the road. But Cass invited me to stay and eat dinner with the two of you before checking in."

"Oh." She kept her expression carefully blank, fully aware she should want to see the last of Knox. Not feel this gladness that they'd have yet more hours together.

"I'm convinced he's still in the process of checking me out."

"You could just tell Dad you're not interested in me."

"No can do, darlin'." Knox shook his head. "I'm certain that he, if not those dogs, can sniff out a lie."

She frowned at him. "You say the most disconcerting things."

He shrugged, his gaze trained on her face. "You can tell me not to stay, Erin. I'll make up an excuse for Cass."

She hesitated, not entirely surprised by her father's kindness to a stranger, but unsure of it, too. What was his agenda? Could Knox be right, and her dad had sensed something between them?

A something that wasn't to be, she reminded herself firmly.

The simplest solution to the problem was to encourage Knox to white-lie his way out of dinner. They could say yet another goodbye, and she'd steer clear of the repair business until she was certain he'd turned his bike northward.

"Your call," Knox said.

Her mind warred with that other part of her that he'd awakened at the Moonstone Café the night before. The woman in her who suddenly remembered what it was like to flirt, to laugh, to feel desired.

To kiss.

"Erin?"

Instead of answering the question at hand she posed her own. "Your dad. Does he want to approve of the women you involve yourself with?"

"My dad." He dropped his head to study the toes of his boots. "We weren't close."

Weren't close. A new emotion entered the small room. Erin tried to sense what Knox wasn't saying. She drew closer to him. "He's...he's passed away, then?"

"Yeah." He cleared his throat. "A few months back, from a rare cancer. I have six brothers, but he didn't tell a single one of us he was dying. Though our mother has been gone for years, we just got a call from her sister after he died. He didn't want a funeral. He didn't want anything from us to recognize his passing."

"That's hard."

"I'm okay with it, though." One hand ran through his dark hair. "It's fine, all of it. We weren't close, like I said."

Without thinking, Erin reached for Knox's hand and held it between both of her own. "I'm sorry. I'm so sorry for your loss."

He stared, unseeing, at their clasped fingers. "He left me the motorcycle, but not a word about why. I'm only guessing he wanted me to go on this ride."

"Well, in any case you need to build up your strength for the open road in your future," she said, certain of her decision now. "Stay for a hot meal. I make amazing chili. My cornbread will break your heart."

"I have this odd premonition that something's going to do that," Knox murmured, still not looking at her.

She wanted to kiss him, hold him, take all that latent hurt she sensed inside him away. "C'mon," she said instead, and began tugging him in the direction of the kitchen. "You can set the table."

The mood lightened as they took their seats before steaming bowls of chili—she didn't tell either man it was vegetarian—and a napkin-covered basket of cornbread. Softened butter waited in another dish.

Cass, never a big talker, was the first to dig in. But he seemed to be listening as Erin probed Knox about growing up one of seven brothers.

"All a success at what they've chosen to do," Knox said. "Lots of competition between brothers contributed to that, I suppose."

"And you?" Erin took her father's napkin from the table and put it in his lap. Knox, she noted, had much better table manners. "How do you fit in with them?"

He shrugged. "I'm not as driven as the others. I'm the most accomplished surfer. Absolutely the most easy-going. The very best at having fun."

There was a bitter tinge to that last sentence that had Erin's antennae on the rise. But before she could delve deeper, her father joined the conversation.

"You don't seem all that relaxed to me, son," Cass said. "How are you going to occupy yourself while you wait on that Indian part to arrive? I guess you might go stir-crazy."

Knox looked toward the older man, his brows rising. "You have something in mind, Cass? I wish I could claim something beyond the most rudimentary of skills when it comes to motorcycle repair. I don't think I'd be much help to you in the shop."

The older man seemed to consider, his right hand rubbing at his chin. "I could give you a break on the bill if you do some other work I've been putting off."

Erin had the impression that money wasn't Knox's number one worry. But she saw her dad had kindled his interest. "Yeah? What's that?"

"I promised Erin I'd paint the locker rooms at her studio. It should take you a day or so for prep and two coats."

"Dad!" she protested. "I can do that."

"I promised to do it for your birthday." He rubbed his right palm over the knuckles of the other hand. "But with the arthritis acting up…"

"It can wait," she said.

"I'd like it done now. Knox?"

The younger man glanced at Erin. "Uh…"

"It's either that or you can shampoo those five dogs I have out back," her father said, straight-faced. "But I warn you—they don't like water. Or getting clean neither."

Before Erin could release the bubble of startled laughter rising in her throat, Knox held out his hand to her father. "Done."

They shook. "Deal," her father rumbled.

"I was bitten by a beagle as a wee lad," Knox told Erin the next day, standing beside the old VW van he'd apparently borrowed from her father and driven to her studio. It was Sunday afternoon, and her classes were over for the day. "I couldn't chance it."

She rolled her eyes. *Wee lad.* He was so full of it. "If you'd walked outside like I asked, I could have proved the yard is completely empty. There is no pack. Dad owns zero dogs."

He reached inside the van for a bucket filled with a new paint roller, a couple of brushes, and packaged drop cloths that he then pushed into Erin's hands. "Take these, will you?"

His fingers curled around the handles of a primer and a paint can.

"Have you considered I might not want to paint today?" she asked.

"You're not painting today." He set the cans on the ground at his feet to pull the vehicle's sliding door shut. From his back pocket, he withdrew a lightweight cap emblazoned with the logo of a big box hardware store that he settled backward on his head.

Erin sighed. He should have looked ridiculous. Why didn't he look ridiculous? Instead, with that cocky grin he beamed her way, he was the rakish bad boy whose heart every girl dreamed of capturing.

"I'm going to paint. You, darlin', are going to do whatever you do on Sunday afternoons."

"Fine," she muttered, stomping toward the entrance to the studio. He could ply the brushes and the roller, and she'd go upstairs and attend to…to…

Something that would put him from her mind. Something that would keep her away from him.

Inside, she showed him to the male and female locker areas, with their metal cabinets and long benches. Each had a door leading to a restroom.

Knox set down his cans to survey the situation, his hands on his hips. "Okay. I'm gonna wash down the walls first. Then apply a primer coat. I'll finish with the paint color you selected."

"Fine. Sure." She dumped an armful of paint

supplies onto a bench, then added for politeness sake, "Don't hesitate to yell if you have any questions. I'll be right upstairs."

He didn't spare her a glance. "I've got this. You enjoy the rest of the afternoon."

Feeling dismissed and stupidly miffed by it, Erin headed to her living quarters. Today, for the first time, he hadn't gotten too close. There'd been no accidental touches. Not a single time had she caught him looking at her mouth.

Apparently lacking any encouragement on her part—hadn't she'd told him she didn't do one-night stands?—the mutual attraction had sputtered out.

Not that she didn't continue to find him incredibly appealing. Even in an old, grease-stained T-shirt advertising Mickey's Motorcycle Sales & Repair, jeans, and beat-up running shoes, he exuded a masculine charisma that went beyond his handsome features, broad shoulders, and long legs. It was an innate confidence that told a woman he'd be good at everything he attempted—surfing waves, painting walls, having sex.

In her kitchen, she prepared a tall glass of ice water and poured it down her throat, hoping to cool herself, or at least drown her overactive hormones. In the distance, she heard Knox begin to whistle, a man without a care in the world.

She tried not to grind her teeth while she puttered, wiping countertops and inspecting the contents of her fridge.

Then, after pouring herself a second glass of water, she decided Knox might be thirsty, too. Rather than putting herself into one of the too-small rooms with him, she propped open the door at the top of the stairs and yelled down to him. "Knox? Would you like something to drink?"

Not long after, footsteps clattered on the hardwood treads as he ascended. He crossed the threshold and looked around her kitchen. "So this is how it works. You have a staircase from here to your studio."

She nodded. "I have another entrance on the other side of the house that doesn't require going through the class space."

"Nice. Mind if I look around?"

Shaking her head, she reached for a glass and filled it with ice and water. Then she tracked him down in her adjacent living area. It was a generous size, with a white-washed fireplace and wide windows that looked across the highway toward the ocean. Beyond it, a short hall led to two bedrooms, each with its own attached bath.

"Here," she said, presenting him with the glass.

He took it, tipping back his head to down the contents in one go.

Mesmerized, Erin watched the muscles work in his tanned throat. As he caught a last, errant drop on his bottom lip with the back of his hand, his gaze met hers.

"What?" he asked.

Did she look like a guppy, her mouth hanging open and her eyes bulging? Instead of answering, she snatched the empty glass from his hand and returned it to the kitchen. But when he didn't follow her there—and then head back down the stairs as she'd hoped—she was forced to return to his side.

Now he appeared to be scrutinizing the ladder shelf set against one wall. "This is nice," he said over his shoulder, indicating the wooden piece. It was shaped like an inverted V, with five horizontal lengths of wood upon which she'd arranged photos, shells, and other mementos. "Especially this." One long finger ran along the natural edge on the supporting posts. "It's almost lacy. Lightens the whole thing."

The compliment pleased her. "My friends' husbands made it for me for Christmas."

"They work with wood?"

"They work with numbers. But they make furniture on the side."

Now Knox picked up one of the framed photographs. "This has to be your mother."

"Yes." The young woman pictured wore a circlet of flowers in her hair and a peasant-style white dress. "On her wedding day." Before he could ask, she found herself adding, "She's gone, though."

He glanced at her. "I'm sorry. Your mom died?"

"Oh, no." Shame washed over her, as it always did when she had to explain this. "She left me and my dad a long time ago. As far as I know she's alive and well."

Knox carefully placed the photo back on the shelf. "Ah."

Apparently I'm remarkably easy to walk away from. "I was a toddler when she took off, leaving nothing but a note behind. She'd been backpacking cross-country when she met my dad and on an impulse married him in Las Vegas after a two-day acquaintance."

"Well." Knox's eyebrows rose. "Cass must have been smitten."

"It seems so. He says she was a light-hearted free spirit, always up for a party or anything new. And then…" Erin shrugged.

"And then?"

She shrugged again. "I guess motherhood became a drag for the free spirit. No fun at all."

Knox's expression softened and he moved closer to Erin, close enough that if she had all the time in the world she could count every one of his lush lashes. "You don't hear from her?"

"On occasion I get cards."

"Yeah?" He reached out to cup her cheek in his broad hand and traced her skin with the edge of his thumb. "Why does that make you cry?"

Lifting her hand, she felt the wetness on her face. Mortified, she stepped away from his touch and wiped away the unexpected moisture. "I didn't realize…I don't know…"

"Erin?" he asked, his voice gentle.

"Sometimes she remembers to send me birthday cards," she said, the words bursting forth from some hidden place where she'd bottled them. "This is not one of those years."

"Oh, darlin'." Knox reached toward her again, this time stroking her hair. "Are you disappointed or are you worried?"

"A little of both, I suppose," she said, then wrapped her arms around herself. "It's stupid. I'm stupid. You'd think I'd grow up sometime and accept she's just not that interested in having a daughter. In me."

Without another word, he gathered her in his arms. Erin jerked back, but he only tightened his hold. After a moment she surrendered, setting her forehead against his shoulder.

"I'm an idiot," she told the cotton of his shirt.

"You're not stupid, and you're not an idiot. In fact, you're successful, beautiful, and kind to strangers who show up on your doorstep looking for help. Not knowing you, not being around you, is your mother's loss."

As she squeezed shut her eyes to hold back more tears, her embarrassment intensified. Did he think she'd been fishing for compliments? "Promise me you'll forget the last few minutes, Knox. I'm usually much more together than this. Actually, I'm usually very together. Inner harmony is sort of my thing."

"You get to be human on occasion, yoga girl."

She felt a light pressure on the top of her head. Had he kissed her there?

Erin looked up. His dark eyes stared into hers, and her pulse scrambled again. Her inner harmony jangled like her nerves, all discordant notes that seemed to crash into each other in the pit of her belly.

"What is this?" she whispered. She couldn't believe she'd confided in him. "What are you doing to me?"

His arms slowly fell away and he stepped away. "I'm not doing my job," he said. "I better get back to the locker rooms."

"Yes." She pulled in a long breath, trying to clear out her confusion. "I…"

He was already halfway across the floor. "What?"

"Nothing." Except she wasn't ready to let him go, even though she knew it was for the best. Safest. The smart thing for the driver of one's own life to allow. "Never mind."

Knox headed for the stairway, and she trailed him at a safe distance. But before he could reach the door—still propped open—she heard noise on the stair treads. Footsteps.

"Hello?" a voice called out. "Erin?"

Deanne and Marissa bustled into the kitchen, then abruptly—almost comically—skidded to a halt when they took in the sight of a man in her home.

"Uh…" Her redheaded friend's eyes widened as her gaze stayed glued to Knox. "Hello there."

Charm came to him so effortlessly. With a smile, he moved forward and held out his hand. "Knox Brannigan."

"I'm Deanne Farmer." She shook his hand then moved aside to indicate her companion. "This is my sister-in-law."

"Marissa," Knox supplied. "Good to meet you. And wow, pregnant women really *do* glow."

Deanne's eyes bugged out, and she shot Erin a look as Marissa beamed and shook hands with Knox.

"You flatter me," Marissa said.

"Call 'em as I see 'em," he replied. "I hope that's a girl in there so she has a chance to inherit her mom's beauty."

Marissa put her hands on her bulging belly. "Thank you," she said with another smile, and Erin could almost guarantee that at this moment she wasn't feeling like anything close to a cow.

Deanne cleared her throat. "So…I remember we saw you at the Moonstone Café. Are you new in town?"

Of course she had to be curious. Erin assumed Marissa had passed on what she'd told her yesterday morning—that she and Knox had gone their separate ways.

"His motorcycle broke down," Erin explained for him. "And it's at Dad's. It's going to take a few days before it's ready to ride again."

"Oooh," Marissa said. "Stuck in a small town, hmm?"

Erin nearly clocked her, pregnant or not. Her imaginative friend was doing it again, casting her and Knox in another movie. "Stuck in a Small Town," part of the Love, Unexpected movie marathon weekend.

"And likely looking for something to pass the time," Deanne added, with a new gleam in her eye.

Uh-oh. Erin gave the redhead a swift once-over. She appeared up to something. "Why are you two here?" she asked.

When Deanne sent a speculative glance at Knox, she jumped in before the woman could answer. "Never mind that right now. Knox, do you need anything before you head down?"

"Not a thing," he said, then turned to Deanne. "How I'm passing the time, you see, is painting Yoga Girl's locker rooms."

"How nice," Marissa said, clasping her hands beneath her breasts. "You need a reward." Her eyes cut to her sister-in-law.

"Exactly what I was thinking," Deanne said. "We dropped by to invite Erin to an impromptu dinner at my place tonight, but now we must include you as well."

Erin opened her mouth to refuse for him. Surely he wouldn't want to attend. He'd feel out of place. Like an afterthought.

Like a charity invite because he had no other better place to be.

Just as she felt so often, the fifth wheel to their tight foursome.

But not tonight, something whispered in her head.

Not tonight with Knox by your side.

"I'd be delighted," he said, before Erin could shush that dangerous voice and dredge up all her objections.

And despite knowing she'd pledged to keep her distance from him, she had to admit to a smidgeon of delight at the idea of the dinner, too.

Chapter 5

Knox paced the perimeter of his utilitarian motel room, killing time before Erin picked him up for the evening with her friends. The gray-brown color of the walls was as dismal as his mood, now that he didn't have a task to keep him busy and no company but his own thoughts. Thank God for the painting job, or he would have had to be elbows-deep in imaginary soap bubbles washing imaginary guard dogs.

Yeah, he'd jumped on that bargain with Erin's dad, Cass, knowing full well there were no vicious—or otherwise—canines. But he'd wanted to do a good turn for the older man...and for Erin, too. Though he knew not to start anything with her, she was still a strong pull for him.

Stronger now, actually, since he'd glimpsed the inner vulnerability hidden beneath her purported inner harmony.

Still, he would continue to resist, remembering

she didn't do one-night stands. She didn't want the only thing he could give her...a fleeting interlude.

The phone he'd purchased that day to replace his broken device buzzed in his pocket. Knox pulled it free and accepted the call, glad of the distraction. "Luke!"

"Hey."

Knox's gut clenched, just for a moment, the timbre of his brother's voice sounding so like their father's. He swallowed. "Hey back. How are you?"

"I'm good. Great, as a matter of fact."

"And how's your beautiful trouble?" Knox asked.

"My what?"

"You don't remember? That's how you described Lizzie to me soon after you re-made her acquaintance."

Luke laughed. "So I did. Now she's just beautiful...and engaged to be my wife."

Knox blinked. Gabe was married, Hunter had taken the plunge and popped the question, and now Luke? "Wow. Best wishes and all that. When did this come about?"

"I asked her on New Year's Eve. Kaitlyn helped me arrange a romantic setting in one of the private cabins. She got a kick out of being in on the proposal, I think."

"Sure she did. And Lizzie's the guardian of her orphaned niece, right? This whole husband thing means not only are you going to have a wife, but Kaitlyn will become your teenage daughter, too."

"I hope I'm good with both."

"A guy like you? Who hangs off cliffs by your fingernails? Marriage and fatherhood will be a piece of cake."

"Dad didn't give us much of a role model to go by."

"But he gave you the resort," Knox said, to avoid the subject of Colin Brannigan, "and by extension, the woman of your dreams."

"He gave you a vintage Indian motorcycle, I understand."

"I'm staggered," Knox said, feigning shock. "One of the Brannigan brothers actually reads the Brannigan email chain."

"Shut up, little brother." Luke hesitated. "You've also left home?"

"With my earthly goods in a bandanna tied to a stick I slung over my shoulder."

"Stop being a smartass. We're worried about you, heading off with no particular destination in mind."

"Says the guy who's chased adventure all around the world."

"Okay," Luke said, sounding sheepish. "There is that. But globetrotting was never your dream."

"Maybe I'm out looking for mine now." He stared out the motel room window into the parking lot, a gloomy dusk descending. "I didn't get far if you want to know the truth. The Indian is in for repairs."

"Already? And you found someone who can work on a rare vintage bike?"

"The address of the shop came with the owner's manual. I was headed here anyway, wanting a mechanic to check out the bike and thinking Mickey of Mickey's Motorcycle Sales & Repair might know how Dad came to own it." Thinking somehow that piece of information might enlighten Knox as to why his father had gifted it to him. Had Colin been trying to send the family rebel, the perennial playboy, his unserious second-youngest son a message from beyond the grave?

Or hadn't he bothered?

"Well?" Luke asked now.

"Mickey's dead."

"Ah. So you're just sitting around, huh? Waiting."

The sympathy in his brother's voice didn't sit well with Knox. "All's good. There's a woman."

"Just one?" Luke's tone lightened, and Knox could actually hear the other man's grin. "With you, there's always a woman."

"This time, she's a—wait for it—*yoga instructor*."

Luke laughed. "You smug bastard."

A car pulled in to the parking lot, its headlights sweeping across the blacktop. "Here she is, as a matter of fact. Gotta go."

"Take care, Knox," Luke said. "And leave the yoga instructor smiling."

Which meant, Knox knew, actually leaving her alone.

It proved difficult, because when he climbed into her car he couldn't look away from her. "You curled your hair." It fell down her back in loose waves. "And those are some boots."

Before he closed the door and the overhead light extinguished, he thought he saw her blush. He knew she shrugged.

"I like to dress up when I have a chance."

It was a short ride to the cul-de-sac in nearby Cinnabar where her friends lived in side-by-side houses. He found out that the Farmer brothers, sons of a local construction developer, had taken over their maternal grandfather's certified public accounting business while another, older brother, worked with their father.

"They labored with their dad's crew to build these homes, though, and that same crew gave me a great deal on the remodel of my house to incorporate the yoga studio," Erin said.

Knox followed her up the walk to one of the front doors, admiring the architectural style of the dwellings instead of dwelling on Erin's perfect ass in a pair of tight dark jeans. New construction in California often meant a Mediterranean style with beige stucco walls and red-tiled roofs. These two homes—though with different layouts—had a beach-and-timber thing going. The walls of the outside entry area appeared to be covered in a white bark.

Erin caught him scrutinizing the surfaces and paused in the act of ringing the front bell. "Poplar panels," she said. "You should have Rob and Tom take you to their workshop. They do all sorts of interesting things."

Then the door opened and they were swept inside. The interior of the house had an open design, and they ended up perched on stools bellied up to the large island while the host and hostess—Rob and Deanne—passed out beers and wine and slid platters of appetizers onto the granite surface. Marissa and Tom soon joined them, and the conversation flowed easily.

It didn't keep him from taking a full inventory of Erin, now that he had a good view of the entire picture she made, from her shiny hair to the tips of her polished boots.

Her mouth was rosy-pink, and the blush-colored sweater she wore did some sort of miracle swoopywrap thing that nearly had it sliding off her shoulders and displayed a sweet hint of cleavage. Though he sat close enough to breathe in her light, floral perfume, he kept his breaths shallow and his attention on the brothers who were regaling him with stories of growing up around dangerous construction equipment.

"...there was that time on the site when you were trying to shoot a huge, nasty flying beetle with a nail gun," Tom was saying to Rob.

"Yeah, you almost pierced my ear instead. And then there was that other time..."

Knox recognized the tenor of their exchanges. He and his brothers—on the rare occasions when a few of them could get together—shoveled the same kind of shit at each other. God, listening to the other two made him realize how much he missed them.

A trio of his siblings—Gabe, Hunter, and Luke— had shown up at The Wake in early December, when Hunter needed some boots on his ass to send him back to the woman he so clearly wanted. He'd managed to convince Becka to take him on, making that three of seven Brannigans now paired up. Did that mean the brothers would see each other even less?

Something hitched in Knox's solar plexus— envy?—at the thought that the coupledom gene must have missed him.

"Uh-oh," Tom said, pointing at Knox. "He lost his smile. We're scaring him, Rob."

His brother crossed to the refrigerator for another beer. "We're not as savage as we sound." Then he paused. "Or maybe we are. It comes from growing up with brothers."

"And from working for our dad since we were nine," Tom added. "Love the man, but he's a martinet.

Don't know how Eddie—that's our older brother—
can stand it. We had to get out from under his thumb."

"I know how that is," Knox admitted. "I worked
for my dad for a while, and that flamed out fast."

"Yeah? What did you do?"

He hesitated. Then thought, *what the hell.* It
wasn't a secret. "He ran a media company. I worked
on the television side of things for a very short period
of time."

"Your father…" Tom began, then released a low
whistle. "Wait. Your last name is Brannigan. Your
father is…*was* Colin Brannigan?"

"Right." He could feel all eyes on him and rubbed
the back of his neck.

"He recently died," Tom said. "In late summer? It
was all over the news."

Erin placed her hand on Knox's thigh, and the
others made compassionate noises. It was enough to
necessitate an immediate change of subject. And
venue. He stood. "I heard about a workshop? How
about a tour?"

That successfully rerouted the conversation as
well as the group itself. They all tromped outside to a
large building at the back of the adjoining properties.
Inside were dozens of specialized tools, work
benches, and projects in progress—tables, chairs,
carved cabinets.

"Wow," Knox said, running his hand along the
surface of a long dining table they said was made with
reclaimed lumber. "This is a mere hobby?"

Rob shrugged. "For now. Maybe someday, with a
little capital, we could each run Grandad's CPA
business half-time and devote the other half to this."

Erin wandered to the far side of the room. "Oh,"

she said, looking down at some photos laid out on a bench. "You're framing our photo."

"Almost done, and then you'll each have one." Tom strolled over, and the others followed. "I like the use of the twigs."

So did Knox. The irregular border comprised of natural material suited the three identical 8 x 10s, a picture of three little girls dressed in sneakers and sweats and surrounded by trees.

"My 11th birthday campout," Marissa said, pointing. "That's me, Deanne, and Erin."

"We stayed up all night planning our wedding proposals," Deanne added.

"Wait," Tom said. "I thought it was your *weddings*."

"Nope," his wife said. "We were certain if our groom-to-be proposed the way we dreamed up then we'd be certain of making the right choice."

Erin pointed to Deanne. "Disneyland. During the fireworks show."

"Hey." Rob looked pleased. "I did that right."

Marissa rolled her eyes. "Because I told you what to do."

"And I told you to tell him what to do," Deanne added. "Rissa thought her perfect guy would propose with a puppy."

"There were so many hints," Tom said, "that I couldn't miss it."

"But the dog tag inscribed with 'Marry Me' was your very own idea." Marissa patted his arm. "And now we have our darling Lab, Buster."

Knox looked to Erin. "And you?"

She shook her head. "I don't even remember."

"A bathtub filled with flowers," her two friends

said together.

"Don't ask me why," Erin said, hanging her head. "Clearly I had low expectations in the romance department even then. I should have gone with a trip to Paris or a pony."

Clearly I had low expectations in the romance department even then. For some reason, the comment ate at Knox throughout the rest of the evening. As did something else, that he finally addressed when they'd made it back to his hotel after an excellent dinner shared with pleasant company.

"You didn't seem surprised that my father was Colin Brannigan."

Erin pulled into a parking space and turned off the ignition. The interior of the small car had warmed during the short trip from her friends' house. "I put it together after you talked about your brothers and your recent loss during dinner last night," she said, shrugging. "Like Tom, I remember seeing it on the news."

"You didn't say anything."

"Should I have? Because he was a wealthy and powerful man? That doesn't matter to me. You're the one I know." She cleared her throat. "I'm not suggesting I *know* know you, that sounds presumptuous, but—"

"I get what you're trying to say."

"Whew. Because it was coming out all wrong."

Knox shifted his knees to angle her way. "I like the Farmers. They're good people."

She nodded, a bob of her head that signaled nerves.

He knew why. In the small confines of the car, the electricity generated between them was impossible to ignore. The air was humming.

Tension coiled in his belly and tightened his muscles.

Hardened his dick.

Even from a seat away. Even without touching her.

But he'd decided to play saint and keep his hands and his mouth to himself. *Damn.* He let his head fall against the cushioned rest behind it, knowing he'd spend the rest of the night frustrated and hurting.

Every male instinct he possessed told him she'd be doing the same.

"I want to kiss you," he admitted, his voice low. He couldn't help himself. "I'm dying to kiss you."

He heard her audible swallow. Without looking at her, he was aware she trembled.

"My hands are itching to crawl over your skin," he continued. "I want to discover your heat, your wet. I want to know the flavor of you. Your nipples. The taste of you between your thighs."

Another swallow. A short pant. "W-why are you saying this?"

"Because despite my best efforts not to, I'm considering a seduction, darlin'." Despite the fact that it might only underscore those low romantic expectations of hers. "If I decide to go in that direction, you're free to refuse me, of course, but fair warning."

"Fair warning?" she echoed faintly.

"I'll try my very best to persuade you to take a little walk on the wild side. To take a little walk with the rebel inside me."

"Knox…"

He reached for the door handle, levered it down

so it swung open, letting in a blast of bracing night air. "Take tonight to think over your response. If I do decide to try coaxing you into bed with me, you need to figure out whether you truly want to deny yourself."

While taking yoga class, Erin urged her students to quiet their minds through smooth movement and something they called ujjayi breathing, in that way disconnecting from day-to-day annoyances and ordinary cares for fifty minutes. But as she finished leading her late-morning Monday practice, she knew this time the teacher had been no example for her pupils.

During each pose, her thoughts had been consumed by Knox. Well, by what he'd said the night before.

If I decide to try coaxing you into bed with me, you need to figure out whether you truly want to deny yourself.

What decision had he come to? And what would her response be if he did, indeed, attempt a seduction?

He'd been to the studio that morning, during an earlier class, when he'd unobtrusively slipped into one of the locker rooms to continue working. He'd slipped out just as quietly, giving her no indication of what he'd settled on.

But more of his words continued to drift through her head like smoke.

I want to kiss you. I'm dying to kiss you.

My hands are itching to crawl over your skin. I want to discover your heat, your wet. I want to know the flavor of you. Your nipples. The taste of you between your thighs.

A shiver rolled down her spine as she came to her feet. Then, while mats were rolled and bare toes were slipped into shoes, she made her way to the studio entrance to bid the class members goodbye. As the first exited, she noted the pleasant temperature of the sun-laden air—they were having a warm spell—and propped open the door.

One by one her students exited, until the final pupil paused in the patch of yellow sunshine cast on the wood floor. Lindsay Fox, who took an early lunch from her admin job at the large spa-resort a few miles south, tucked her mat under her arm. "Your yoga class almost makes me look forward to Mondays."

"That's quite a compliment," Erin said, smiling at the other woman. "I'm glad you enjoyed it."

And that you didn't notice my distraction. "Have a great rest of your day, Lindsay."

"I just might," the other woman said, nodding over Erin's shoulder. "With the memory of that inspiring sight to brighten my afternoon."

She glanced around and saw Knox had returned. In the parking lot, he leaned against the front of the old VW van, legs crossed at the ankles, arms relaxed. His eyes on her.

I want to kiss you. I'm dying to kiss you.

"Oh. Well." A blush crawled up her neck.

"Friend?" Lindsay asked, waggling her brows.

"Just a guy doing some work for me," she answered, well aware Knox could hear every word. "He probably has a question or something."

"Speaking of work," Lindsay said. "I've had an idea."

"Okay…?"

"What if you came to the spa and taught some

classes there each week? Now we direct guests to your studio, and certainly many make the trip, but you might get more clients if you came to us."

Erin tilted her head, wondering about the logistics. "You have the space?"

"We could make the space. And in good weather you could hold class on the lawn or even on our beach. I know that would be a hit."

"It's an intriguing offer," Erin said. "Let me give it some thought."

"I'll think some more, too. I mentioned it to my boss and she was very interested. We'll talk about how many sessions we think we could fill. Maybe create some special events too."

"Okay. Let me know." Erin smiled again. "Thanks. And thanks for the consideration."

Lindsay strolled out the door then, not even trying to hide the long, admiring look she sent Knox. Grinning, he gave her a nod, then pushed off the van to saunter, loose-hipped and lazy, toward Erin.

"'Morning, teach."

"Good morning." She checked the clock. "Well, it's nearly afternoon."

"Yeah. Lunchtime. I see on the posted schedule that you have a break until three."

"That's right." Just the way he was looking at her made her skin tighten on her bones. She cleared her throat. "Um—"

"Are you going to do it?"

Did he mean go to bed with him? *Sheesh.* What happened to seduction? Licking her lips, she stalled for time. "Do, um, what?"

"Hold some yoga sessions at the spa like that woman mentioned. Seems a natural way to branch out."

Okay, not seduction. He wanted to talk about business. She made a face. "I don't know. I'll see how many sessions they want to offer, what else they have in mind. There are only so many hours in the day."

"You lead all the classes yourself now?"

"I do."

He frowned. "What about when you take a vacation?"

"Vacation?" She cocked her head, as if it was a brand new concept. "What's that word?"

His frown deepened. "All work, no play, Erin."

"It takes a lot of energy and focus to get a new business off the ground," she said, her tone defensive. Because his comment reminded her of what Deanne had said recently. *Now it's time for the yoga girl to have a little fun again.*

"Things are solid at the studio?"

She shrugged, nodded.

"So now you get some other instructors on the payroll. Consider those classes at the resort. You should have some branded clothing to sell here, by the way, and I bet the resort gift shop would stock it as well if you taught there. Your logo's a winner." His gaze shifted to where Yoga Girl was painted on an interior wall, the "o" a yellow sun with spiked rays, a blue crescent moon hanging off the bottom curve of the second "G."

"I came up with it myself."

"Good eye."

She ignored her flush of pleasure. "For a part-time bartender, you sound like you know something more than how to make a mai tai."

"In a shaker, pour one ounce each of lime juice,

Martinique rum, and dark Jamaican rum. Add half an ounce of orange Curaçao, another of orgeat, then one-fourth ounce of sugar syrup. Next comes crushed ice, fifteen seconds of shaking, and then pour the mixture into a double old-fashioned glass. Garnish with mint." He shoved his hands into the pockets of his battered jeans, now with a few paint spatters here and there. "But I also have an MBA. I specialized in entrepreneurship."

She blinked.

His smile was self-deprecating. "And here you thought I was just some guy with hay between his ears instead of brains."

"I didn't say that." She crossed her arms over her chest. "And I didn't think that."

"You're cute when you're indignant," he said, and flicked the tip of her nose with his finger. "Ready for lunch?"

"Oh. Well…" The quick switch of topics flustered her.

"I brought a picnic. I thought we could eat it on the beach."

Did he plan his seduction on the sand? Or was this just a friendly gesture, and he'd decided he didn't want her after all? She bit her lip. "I have paperwork…"

"All work, no play, darlin'," he said, and slapped his hands together. "Let's get some shoes on you and lock up."

And just like that, instead of taking off her clothes, he had her putting more on. Socks, sneakers, and then a zip-up sweatshirt. "I thought we could walk," he said.

"If we're careful, we can run across the highway

right here." She watched him pull from the van a beat-up leather backpack that had a baguette sticking out the top and a striped blanket, rolled tight, tied below. "But we can't cross the railroad tracks."

He glanced at her as he slid the door shut. "Why not?"

"Because it's...it's a rule."

"Made to be broken," he said, shouldering the pack.

Another shiver tumbled down Erin's spine. *I'll try my very best to persuade you to take a little walk on the wild side. To take a little walk with the rebel inside me.*

It shouldn't sound so enticing. "Um…"

While she continued to mentally dither, he merely grabbed her hand in a no-nonsense grip and began walking.

It was a moment's effort to sprint across the blacktop of the two lanes of highway. Then they trudged through grasses and iceplant to reach a portion of track that sat atop a seventy-five-yard-long trestle. "See," Erin said, pointing. "We can't just hop over them. We have to pick our way along the ties until we can jump down on that berm over there."

"We can do it." Knox glanced in both directions, then squeezed her hand. "Let's go."

She dug in her heels. "Knox…"

"Wild side, babe," he said, then began towing her forward.

Her reluctance felt silly once they safely had traversed the piece of track and found their feet in the sand. He looked down at her. "You okay?"

A bit breathless, but that could be because he still held her hand. And because of that striped Mexican blanket strapped to his backpack. On a weekday, on this stretch of coastline, they had the beach to themselves. It was breezy, but the sun was warm, and if they found shelter behind one of the many dunes, they wouldn't freeze if he decided to—

But had he made that decision?

And what was hers?

"I'm okay," she said, swallowing hard.

Then he was towing her again, until he came upon a smooth stretch of sand between two five-foot mounds topped with long, dried grasses. Instant privacy.

Her heart started to pound as he dropped her hand and went about freeing the blanket. With the flick of his wrists he unfurled it then spread it flat, a fringed oasis of red, blue, and green. Standing at one edge, he toed off his running shoes then peeled away his socks.

He raised an eyebrow in her direction. "Ready?"

For what? But then he dropped onto the striped covering and she didn't know what to say or do besides remove her own footwear so she wouldn't track sand either.

He patted the space beside him. "Get comfortable."

Feeling self-conscious, she dropped to her knees and crawled to where he indicated, hoping no scratchy particles made their way onto the fabric surface. They could be uncomfortable later if they found their way into certain personal spaces...

Wait a minute.

Was she really considering having sex with Knox Brannigan? But it seemed some of her was, anyway, because her heart continued to slam against her ribs and the shivers running over her skin felt more like thrill than reluctance.

Planting her butt on the blanket, she sat up straight, her fingers going to the zipper of her sweatshirt. In this sheltered location, it was much too hot for an extra layer of clothes.

The sound of the metal teeth parting was loud, even over the constant *shush* of the waves. Knox glanced over and her hand froze, poised between her collarbone and cleavage.

Did he think she was rushing to the undressing?

"Good idea," he said, and, reaching for the hem of his own pullover sweatshirt, yanked it over his head. The T-shirt underneath rode up with his movement, revealing a slice of tanned, rippled abdominal muscles.

Her mouth went dry. *Oh, God.*

She'd gone without touching or being touched by a man for six years. Getting close to one such as this might cause her to go up in flames before either of them got fully undressed. She'd *told* Deanne that she needed a tame first ride following her spell of celibacy. Knox was anything but. He was a high-octane machine, sleek and powerful and capable of speeds and maneuvers outside of her experience or abilities.

How gauche would she appear if she made some excuse and took off running for home?

"Erin?" Knox tossed his sweatshirt aside. "You haven't moved. Do you need help with that zipper? Is it stuck?"

"I...uh..."

While she searched for an answer, he scooted closer and brushed her hand away. Then he grasped the metal pull. As he eased it down, he lifted his gaze to hers.

"I think you need to breathe, darlin'."

She did her best, taking in short pulls of air as he parted the two sides of the fleece. His hands went inside the garment to cup her shoulders, bared by the stretchy tank top she'd worn for yoga class. He swept his palms down her arms, igniting nerves as he stroked her naked skin.

The sweatshirt bunched at her wrists, and he took hold of the ribbing of her right sleeve and slowly worked it over her hand. He did the same on the left side, the innocuous action seeming excruciatingly intimate to her hyper-aware self. When she was finally freed, he lobbed the fleece toward his. It settled on top, for all the world looking like a lover snuggled up to her mate.

Or maybe that was just Erin's hormonally influenced imagination.

Wearing a small smile, Knox studied her face. His hand reached for the strap of his backpack and drew it closer. Then he flipped back the top and reached inside, rustling around.

What was he seeking? A condom? Surely he would have a condom.

Then his arm was withdrawing. She stared as it emerged from the mouth of the pack.

Chapter 6

Knox offered Erin the clear bag he cradled in the palm of his hand. "Grapes?"

Her wide eyes shifted from the fruit to his face and then she burst out laughing, her body flopping full-length onto the blanket.

Now it was his turn to stare, bemused, as she continued giggling, her arms crossing her flat belly as if it hurt. He leaned over her, fascinated by the amusement lighting her face. For once, her wariness around him had dissolved completely.

"Do I want to know what you find so funny?" he asked, his own grin twitching the corners of his mouth.

"No," she choked out, her head moving from side to side. It loosened the bun on the top of her head, and he tucked his finger under the band to release the coil of her hair.

She didn't seem to notice as her giggles slowly

subsided.

"No?" he asked again.

"No." When she sat up again, her silky hair slid in shiny strands around her shoulders.

He wasn't going to push for an answer right now. A man with his experience knew when to hold back.

It was his intention to go slowly with the seduction as well. An attempt to persuade her into sex was inevitable—another night of craving her had proved that he wanted her almost beyond reason, and he was, frankly, unpracticed at denying himself—but pouncing wasn't his style. So he'd hit upon the idea of a casual lunch as an appetizer before the entrée and dessert that would be their bodies, a bed, and hours of exploration.

She plucked the grape bag from his hand now, opening it to pop some of the fruits free of their vine. Her cheeks puffed like a chipmunk's as she filled her mouth.

He laughed. "Greedy thing."

Silver eyes dancing, she chewed with relish. A trickle of juice escaped the seam of her lips, and he found the sight so erotic he hastily looked away before his own greed got him into trouble. God, he wanted his hands on her. Bad.

But moving too fast wasn't the way.

So he turned his attention to the provisions inside his backpack, drawing out each item and placing it on the blanket between them—a plastic container of plump, marinated olives, a wedge of Brie, the baguette, and then a packet of thick, chocolate chip-and-walnut cookies.

She grabbed them up. "Did you get these at Bonnie's Bakery?"

"I did," he said, taking them back. "But sweets don't come first."

"What?" Erin pouted, which he found adorable. "*Now* you want to follow rules?"

"Steps, darlin'. One thing at a time." He passed her a small wooden cutting board and a knife, withdrew a packet of sliced salami, and then nudged the loaf of bread in her direction. "You make the sandwiches."

Keeping her busy would keep any residual nerves at bay. Confident he was on the right track with her, he leaned back on his elbows to watch her slice and arrange, every movement of her delicate hands graceful.

He wanted to feel them on his skin. He wanted to draw each slender finger into the wet heat of his mouth and suck on iy, running his tongue over the sensitive inner surfaces until he felt her shiver and heard her moan.

She glanced up at him, a quick flash of silver from beneath her lashes. "I suppose you've been on a lot of picnics."

"My share." Knowing what she was getting at, his lips twitched. "But every single one of them is different. Special in its own way."

One of the sandwiches went on a napkin he'd also unpacked, and she passed it over. "I'm not as much of a picnicker as you. As a matter of fact, I haven't shared an…an outdoor meal in some time."

"It doesn't require vast experience," he assured her smoothly, trying not to laugh again. *Outdoor meal.* "Only enthusiasm. I think I can help you with that."

Rolling her eyes, she shook her head. "You."

"Hey," he protested. "I didn't start the metaphor."

"But you brought the food."

He groaned. "I don't know where to go with that. Can we just enjoy lunch?"

She sent him another quick look. "Oh, all right. Pass the olives."

They demolished nearly everything. At the end of their feast only a small curve of sourdough crust remained, and a lonely trio of olives. The rest was a mere memory, including the bottles of water he'd also provided.

With the leftovers and trash stowed in the backpack, he stretched out on the blanket and closed his eyes. After a moment, he sensed her doing the same.

Turning his head, he studied her beautiful face, her dark lashes fanned against her cheekbones. She looked as replete as he felt, but he suspected there also ran through her veins the same hum of anticipation that he was experiencing.

Smiling, he savored that sweet knife-edge of keen sexual arousal awaiting its unleashing. The "before" interlude had its own charms and was one of his favorite steps in the game of mating.

Though her eyes remained closed, Erin's rosy lips parted. "MBA, huh?"

"Yeah, earned it part-time a couple of years ago," he said, not sure if he regretted telling her. His brothers didn't even know about it. "I got my bachelors at the University of California at Santa Barbara. Double-majored in beer and surfing."

She made a scoffing noise. "What did you really major in?"

"Econ," he admitted, surprised she didn't just let

the bullshit go. "You know, most people look at me and swallow 'beach bum' hook, line, and sinker. Including my family, by the way."

"Why would you want to give them that impression in the first place?"

To fulfill expectations. Colin Brannigan had come to label his second-youngest son as unserious and irreverent.

And Knox used his laid-back image to decrease expectations, too. With six brothers cutting wide swathes in worlds that ran from high finance to adventure filmmaking, Knox didn't want his own pursuits compared to their accomplishments.

"I don't know," he muttered now.

"So, you wanted to go to work in a suit and tie," Erin said. "Interesting."

Now it was his turn to scoff. "The suit and tie were never the draw."

"No?"

"And I really *do* like to surf," he said. "It's a passion."

"Still…" she said, "Econ. MBA. You don't need those to learn to shred the waves."

"I could shred the waves when I was ten," he said. "I went for those degrees because…" What was he doing? This kind of soul-searching and heavy conversation he engaged in with exactly…nobody.

He glanced over at Erin to see her eyes open now, the expression in them calm. Waiting. Non-judgmental.

"All those brothers," he heard himself say. "Each one of them knew what he wanted, and none of them wanted to do whatever that was under our father's thumb. Even Perfect James, who was probably closest to him, had enough of Dad as boss after being expected to oversee his six younger siblings for years."

"So you thought you'd be the one to work with him?"

"I briefly made the attempt when I was twenty-one. After college."

"Briefly?"

Knox threw his forearm over his eyes. "Yeah. When I was still young enough to want to win his approval. When I was naïve enough to think he would ever give me that."

"You clashed then?"

"Brutally. Often. Maybe if he'd let me start in the mail room like I asked—"

"Are there still mail rooms in companies?"

"Of a sort. Anyway, he didn't like anything I did." He laughed a little, the sound bitter. "Those last six words sum up the entire relationship."

A small hand crept into the free one resting at his side. Erin squeezed his fingers. "I'm sorry."

"He thought I never took anything seriously," Knox said, trying to breathe despite a tightness constricting his lungs.

Her hand continued to clasp his.

"So I made sure it looked exactly like that on the outside, once I quit." He let his arm fall from his eyes to stare up at the sky, a blue so flat it appeared ironed.

"Hence the beach bum image."

"And the part-time bartending."

"You don't know how to make a mai tai?" she sounded crestfallen.

He laughed as he thought she meant him to, the chains around his chest easing a little. "No, I do. And

I take regular shifts to help out. But I invested in that bar with a friend."

Erin's gaze narrowed. "*With* a friend or *for* a friend?"

Sitting up, Knox shrugged. "Turns out to be the same, since we make bank."

Now she shifted position, sitting up too and mimicking his pose so both their knees were drawn up, their feet toes-to-toes. "What else?" she asked.

His brows rose. "Uh…"

"What else have you invested in?"

"Well…"

She snapped her fingers. "The card game. *Greetings from an Admirer*. Did you put up some cash for that?"

How had she guessed? "I might have. Very little."

Erin's head tilted. "How do you find people who need…what do they call them? An angel investor?"

Reaching out, he tucked a strand of her hair behind her ear. "Now, you know I'm no angel, darlin'."

She narrowed her eyes. "Knox."

"Okay, okay. I keep in contact with one of my profs from business school. He hears of things. Small stuff. Steers interesting proposals my way. And I know a lot of people who introduce me to other people." Smiling, he tickled her toes with his own. "So I own part of a shoelace company. Very trendy shoelaces. And a surf shop."

"Your dad didn't know any of this? What about your brothers?"

Knox shook his head. "My brothers are busy with their own interests. And Colin would have considered the mom-and-pop style enterprises I put my money into a waste of time. He was more a go big or go home type of guy."

"But what you do is big," she said, her brows cinching together over her small nose. "Really, really big."

Bemused, he gazed into her earnest face. "You think so?"

"I know so." She leaned toward him. "Knox, don't you see? You give people their dreams."

He froze, an instant denial stuck in his throat. *You give people their dreams.*

The words unsettled him, signaling an intimacy he hadn't invited. Didn't want.

"I...uh..." Stymied, he looked away and reached for his backpack. "It's getting late."

Too late, a voice inside him whispered. *This woman sees you. She sees something inside you that your father would never appreciate and your brothers would never imagine.*

Erin glanced down at the slim sports watch on her wrist. "Yikes. We've got to hurry. I've got to prepare for my next class."

As they gathered up the picnic things, she chattered about inconsequential matters, and Knox found his tension easing. When she bent to lift the blanket off the sand, he gazed on her great ass and felt the familiar rise of lust—something he knew quite well how to handle.

Yeah, back to well-known territory.

Dinner, he decided. He'd suggest bringing groceries to her place tonight where he'd make them a meal. And then have dessert in bed.

It was time—all his instincts told him she was as

interested as he. Tossing the pack onto his back, he followed Erin as she led the way toward the trestle. She hurried, almost floating over the surface of the sand, and he smiled at the image she made—a bright butterfly flitting through the sunshine-and-salt laden air.

His spirits buoyed higher as he watched her clamber onto the railroad tracks. The gloom he'd seemed to be carrying around lately now gone.

Go, sex, he thought, grinning. A shag with the yoga girl and he'd be back to his old self, slinging drinks, shredding surf, and keeping things light.

He glanced over his shoulder at the ocean, watching the small waves form and fold, form and fold. *All's right. All's right with the—*

Then he heard it, ominous as thunder. Wheels rumbling on a steel track.

His heart shoved to his throat, and he whipped around to see that Erin was two-thirds of the way along the trestle. A monster was barreling toward her, a gigantic, lethal land-eel that would eat a butterfly. Or squash it flat.

God. Please, God.

He leaped onto the tracks. They thrummed beneath the soles of his shoes as he raced toward Erin, his focus on the bright blue of her sweatshirt. Panic and fear pinballed inside him, devastating everything in their paths, demolishing all his defenses, creating jagged splinters that slashed great tears in his easy-come, easy-go, what's-to-get-riled-about approach to life.

The train's whistle screamed, or maybe that was him.

His eyes burned, his lungs burned. They weren't

going to make it.

They had to make it.

With a desperate leap, he flung himself toward Erin, throwing his arms around her body, and using his momentum to propel them both over the side of the trestle. They landed with a thump, a fall of maybe five feet, and they lay there, plastered together, as the land-eel sped past.

Euphoria chased the adrenaline rushing through him as Knox, shaking, pressed his face to Erin's hair and breathed in its scent in ragged gulps. They were okay. She was fine.

They were okay, he repeated to himself. She was fine.

But those thoughts faded away as she turned in his arms and he looked into her beautiful face.

She could have been killed.

Her cheeks flushed, Erin stared at him with wide eyes. "Scary."

Unwilling to trust he still had a voice, he nodded, tightening his arms around her slender frame.

Her hand reached up to touch his cheek. "Are you all right?"

No. Now that the initial relief had passed, he knew something huge had happened to him. *I almost lost Erin.*

Terror moved through him again, rearranging critical pieces of himself in ways he could never describe. His chest ached, his temples throbbed, nausea filled his twisted gut. His bones rattled under his skin.

Oh, God. I almost lost Erin.

Anguish wrapped a fist around his heart and squeezed until it bled.

Nothing had ever hurt like this before.

Perhaps the train had hit him after all and this was hell.

"I was never so scared in my life, Deanne." Erin held her phone to her ear with one hand and towel-dried her hair with the other. "I thought we were going to die."

"And you could have," her friend said, scolding. "That's a terrible place to cross."

Erin nodded, even though the other woman couldn't see the movement. "My hands were still shaking when I started my next class."

"You won't forget that experience."

For more than one reason. "The thing is…" Erin hesitated. "Um…"

"What?"

"I also never felt so alive."

"What?" Deanne squawked. "When you almost became train-kill?"

"No," Erin said, thinking back. It was the time spent with Knox, being around his vitality, his charm, his smoldering sexuality. Though his fire had been banked during their picnic, she'd sensed his heat beneath the surface. "It's him. Knox. He makes me…fully alert. Aware of everything." Her heartbeat. The tang of the salty air on her tongue. The way his palms lit every nerve as he drew them down her bare arms.

She tossed her towel into the hamper and picked up a comb. "The girl-meets-train near miss was just some danger frosting on the cake."

Deanne groaned. "Maybe Rissa and I should have kept quiet on your birthday. We created a monster. A monster hungry for danger-frosted cake named Knox. Didn't you say you needed tame?"

Somehow, though, the want of him had subdued her misgivings. "Come on, Deanne. You think he's nice. The husbands liked him."

"Yeah," the other woman said, "but he's passing through. He told you that. He told all of us that."

Erin stared at her reflection in the mirror over her dresser. Her eyes appeared brighter with her face flushed from a hot shower. Beneath her thin terry robe, her skin twitched, her flesh so sensitive that the soft fabric seemed to chafe. *It's time to put yourself out there. Open up. Loosen up.*

"Did you hear me, Erin? He'll be gone soon."

She pulled in a deep breath and cast a glance toward the windows. Darkness had settled over her house, but inside her something new glowed, brightening what she saw now had become a dull, too-mundane life. "Maybe that means I don't have any time to waste."

Things to do.

At Deanne's surprised gasp, Erin ended the call.

She dried her hair. Donned her best underwear, then pulled on an oversized flannel shirt and leggings. As she struggled into a pair of knee-high sheepskin boots, she frowned. They'd be as difficult to strip off as they were to get on, right?

She exchanged them for ankle-skimming leather booties with short side zippers. Her heart bobbed in her chest as she inspected her outfit in the mirror. When was the last time she'd dressed for a man?

The act made her feel young and vulnerable...and so excited that her hands started to tremble again. Shaking them out, she headed for the makeup drawer in the bathroom where she hoped her heavy duty mascara hadn't dried up from lack of use.

She hoped *she* hadn't dried up from lack of use.

Features enhanced by her meager supply of cosmetics, she now gathered her purse and a jacket. Keys next. When she and Knox had made it back to the yoga studio that afternoon, some early students had been waiting, precluding a chance for private conversation. They'd not made any future plans.

But she knew the way to where he was staying. Finding his room should be a snap.

Armed with a cold six-pack of craft beer, she stepped from her car onto the cracked surface of the parking lot of the Rest Ezy Motel. She glanced around, taking in the two stucco stories, with spaces for vehicles aligned in front of the first-floor doors. The aroma of pizza drifted through the air.

Maybe she and Knox could order one to be delivered. After.

Her gaze settled on her dad's old VW, parked in front of room 104, and she swallowed hard. Knox, her chance to walk on that wild side he'd promised, was just a few footsteps away.

Take a little walk with the rebel inside me.

It was those glimpses of the interior of him that intrigued her as much as the appealing outside package. There was a rebel there, she saw that, but he was also a canny businessman, a caring friend, and a son grappling with a fresh loss.

But she wasn't here to plumb the depths of his soul, she reminded herself, taking a firmer grip on the beer carton. She didn't have time for that. It wasn't the purpose of their association. Tonight she simply wanted to end a six-year stretch of celibacy with a man who could make her burn with a single glance.

Room 104.

Blackout curtains covered the double-wide windows, though a slim line of yellow light leaked at their center. No sound reached her ears, but she thought the light and the van were evidence that Knox was within.

She stood in front of the door and trained her gaze on the beady eye of the peephole. Then, squaring her shoulders, she knocked.

The night's normal sounds disappeared. The rush of tires along the bordering road, the *tick-tick-tick* of an engine cooling nearby, the hum of the Rest Ezy's neon sign—V CANCY—now overridden by the loud thump of her heart in her ears. As the seconds stretched on, Erin placed her free hand against her chest and tried massaging the undisciplined organ inside.

Yet the door still remained closed.

She glanced around, wondering if he'd gone for a walk or out for food or if he stood under the spray of the shower, naked and wet, his big hand spreading soap lather over his pecs so that bubbles arrowed in twin trails to his groin.

Swallowing a moan, she knocked louder.

He'd hear that, wouldn't he? Then turn off the water, sling a notoriously skimpy motel towel around his hips. It would take him eleven seconds to cross the rug and put his eye to the peephole.

He'd open the door in three…two…one.

Nothing happened.

Okay. *He's out walking then.* She spun around, searching the area, then spun back. Or maybe not Room 104, she thought, lifting her gaze. 204?

There were concrete stairs at the end of the building. Her heels clattered against their surface, and she steadied herself by grasping the wrought-iron railing, pitted with rust. With a scowl of distaste, she wiped her gritty palm on the long tail of her shirt. If she'd had his cell number she would have called and invited him to her place.

Room 204 turned out to be another bust. No light peeped between the curtain edges. The door went unanswered.

Dejected, Erin descended the steps to the first level. She considered returning to her house, alone. Then she recalled the sensation of Knox's strong arms around her. *Not giving up yet.*

Her gaze wandered to the motel's tiny office. With her dad living and working just down the street, she didn't feel like advertising to the clerk she was seeking a single male guest. In a small community such as this one, word could get back to Cass.

She looked at the van Knox had been driving again. Okay. Not Room 104. Not 204. But what about 105 or 106 or…?

With renewed resolve, she marched up to 105. Definitely occupied, because she could hear the TV from the other side of the door. Hauling in a deep breath—and telling herself that the third time was the charm—she rapped on the painted surface.

After a moment, it swung open releasing bright light, the sound of *Monday Night Football*, and a man she hadn't seen in six years.

Erin gaped. "Wiley?"

His lean body was dressed in jeans and a T-shirt advertising an Austin rodeo. He was in stocking feet, but she could see his scuffed cowboy boots, tumbled behind him in the middle of the floor.

His gaze ran over her, and he scratched at the stubble on his chin. "Uh…"

Humiliation warred with fury. He didn't remember her!

"Beer delivery?" he asked in a hopeful tone.

"No." She backed away. "Not a beer delivery, but a big blunder."

Just then his hand snaked out, and he caught her arm. "Wait, wait. *Erin*?" His eyes narrowed. "Erin Cassidy? Is it you?"

"Yes," she hissed, tugging to free herself from his hold.

"Wow." His grip didn't loosen. "You're even more beautiful now. I've been in the area a couple weeks—helping my aunt clean out her place now that she's widowed—and I never thought you might still be around."

"You might recall I'm from here," she said, through gritted teeth. "And I came back here after you left me hundreds of miles north without gas or cash." Only with the ridiculous "engagement ring" he'd fashioned out of the foil he'd peeled off a bottle of beer. Then, because she couldn't help herself, she added. "I hope your aunt's doing okay."

Dropping his hand from Erin's arm, he nodded. "Gettin' better." Then he rubbed his chin again. "About that gas and cash…"

"Never mind," she said stiffly. "Just forget about it."

He reached for her again, this time taking her hand in one of his. "Sweetheart," he said, with a little smile that she remembered him wearing while they two-stepped around the dance floor at the country bar where they'd met. His thumb stroked the back of her hand. "Maybe I can make it up to you."

Make up for abandoning her and crushing her hopeful, hapless heart? She didn't think so.

Her voice rose. "Not going to happen. Now, if you'd return my hand?"

"I remember the way it felt on my skin those days and nights we had together."

Those days and nights during which she thought they were planning to be "together" forever. She wanted to slap his handsome face and then stomp on his stocking-covered toes. "Let me go, Wiley."

"Erin?"

Her head whipped around to see Knox strolling down the walkway, the door to Room 103 open behind him.

103. She nearly slapped her palm to her forehead.

Then he was standing beside her. His gaze traveled from Wiley to where the other man's hand joined with Erin's.

She attempted a discreet tug. He didn't release her.

"Who's this?" Knox asked, his expression cool.

"An old friend, Wiley Jones," Wiley answered for her. "And we're about to get reacquainted. My lucky night."

"We're *not* getting reacquainted."

Knox's brows rose. "You brought him beer."

"I knocked on the wrong door."

Those dark arches rose higher. "Is that right?"

"Like I said, my lucky night," Wiley put in. "We knew each other…what? Five? Six years ago?"

This time she yanked so hard to repossess her hand that when he let go, she fell back a step. Knox caught her, bringing her against his body to nuzzle her temple.

"Darlin'," he murmured in greeting.

He smelled of soap and his hair was damp, and she realized he'd had a recent shower, just like she'd fantasized.

"Give me your number," Wiley said, gaze on her.

Knox's answer was instant. "I don't think so."

Wiley's eyes shifted, and his expression betrayed annoyance. "I'm not talking to you."

"Well, I'm talking to you," Knox said, drawing her closer with an arm around her waist. "And Erin's not giving you her number."

She glanced over her shoulder at him, eyes wide. That sounded distinctly…possessive, and he didn't strike her as a possessive kind of man.

"Shouldn't that be her decision?" Wiley challenged.

Knox's set face didn't flicker. "No."

Then he turned Erin and guided her back down the walkway toward Room 103.

"Erin, sweetheart, you know where to find me!" Wiley called after them.

Knox pushed her through his door and shut it with a very final slam. She supposed that was a good enough last word.

But it left her facing a stone-faced man who looked nothing like the smooth charmer she'd become accustomed to. Unsure what to do, Erin crossed to the dresser and deposited the carton of beer on its surface.

"I didn't like him touching you," Knox suddenly said.

She glanced over her shoulder, to see his expression had turned perplexed. "I didn't like it at all," he added darkly.

"I didn't want him to," she offered. "He's...he's an old mistake."

"Good," Knox said, with a return of his usual male smugness. Then his gaze went to the beer. "Are we drinking together?"

"I came over so we could go to bed together," Erin admitted. *Why not?*

Knox stilled and the air went electric.

In response, her nerves rioted. "But," she hastened to add as he began prowling forward, "that run-in with Wiley has killed the mood."

"Really?" Knox's gaze shifted from her eyes to her mouth.

"Really." She realized now that the top button of his jeans was unfastened and that he must have hastily thrown on his shirt, because the pale blue chambray fabric wasn't buttoned at all. The sides fluttered as he advanced, giving her distracting glimpses of tanned skin and taut muscle. Erin pressed her spine to the dresser, the beer bottles clinking against each other like warning chimes.

Still, he got close enough that she could feel his body heat, and her breaths drew in the clean scent of him. One blunt male fingertip reached out and traced the curve of her cheek. Her heart jumped, and goose bumps raced down her neck to fan out beneath her clothes.

Her nipples tightened.

"Killed the mood..." he mused, stroking her face again. "You know, that's an almost irresistible challenge..."

Chapter 7

Knox didn't know what was happening to him. Staring down at Erin, he noted her unsteady breaths and the flush across her cheekbones. Signals that turned his cock to iron and his willpower to mush.

After the incident with the train, he'd decided against getting further involved with her. Not only did she too easily worm her way beneath his boundaries, but those moments of fear for her had thoroughly unsettled him.

Fucked him up.

But then tonight he'd heard her voice beyond his door, a clear note of distress in it, and he'd rushed from his room...

To see another man's hand on her.

Red had filmed over his vision, and he'd barely resisted throwing her over his shoulder and carrying her back to his bed like a caveman with a prize.

Hell. He'd always been smoother than that. More

laid-back.

Now he touched one of her downy eyebrows, following its curve, and realized, in some wonder, that his hand was trembling.

"Yes," he whispered. "I think I'm going to have to put you in the mood again."

Like an otter, she squirmed away from the cage of his body. Standing in the middle of the room she crossed her arms over her chest and glared at him. "I've had enough arrogant male attitude for one night."

Not enough to send her skedaddling to her car. But Knox decided against pointing that out, and instead plucked two of the beers from the carton. He popped the tops, then offered a bottle to her.

Her eyes wary, she came close enough to snatch one away, then retreated again. "What should we drink to?" he asked, considering. "Chance meetings with old mistakes?"

"Never." She pushed out her bottom lip. "That man owes me one-thousand five-hundred and twenty-six dollars, seven gallons of gas, and my self-respect."

"Poor Erin," he murmured, trying to sound calm when all he wanted to do was go back to that other room and take every stolen cent out of that asshole's hide. But he was smart enough to know that would do nothing for the missing self-respect. Or the seduction he had in mind.

Crossing to a chair in the corner, he dropped into it and crossed his legs. "What happened? You staked him in a poker game? Bought his story about a close relative needing a critical operation? Gave him tuition money for stupid school?"

Even that didn't cause a smile. "I agreed to marry

him."

"Oh." Knox blinked, then brought his beer to his mouth for a deep drink.

"Yeah," Erin said, the single syllable full of self-disgust. She tipped her bottle back for her own long swallow.

Knox tilted his head, trying to guess at more particulars. "High school sweetheart?"

"I'd forgive myself for that foolishness." She took another step back to sit on the mattress.

He tried to focus on the discussion at hand instead of what he intended to happen on that surface in the very near future. "So, you were...what age?"

"Twenty-one." She looked away. "We met one Friday night at this local country bar that used to be popular. He was visiting his aunt and uncle."

"And he wooed you to the strains of a Kenny Chesney ballad about old Chevys, tire swings, and summer keg parties."

Her gaze cut to him. "Not a fan of country music?"

"I like all kinds of music. I just don't like the idea of someone hurting you."

She sighed. "I suppose some of the responsibility is my own. We met the next night at the same bar and closed it down, then spent Sunday riding around in his truck. That night, with a huge moon hanging over us like something out of the movies Rissa favors, he told me he'd fallen in love with me. Asked me to marry him. He had a ring."

"A ring?"

"Fine." Erin made a face. "He peeled the label off a beer and molded it from the foil."

"Who can resist a crafty man?"

She laughed, and looked startled that she could. More beer went down her throat, then she told him the rest. The asshole had convinced her to go on the rodeo circuit with him. She'd gathered the tips she'd been saving from her part-time barista job, gassed up her car, and followed him and his truck out of town.

"We stayed in a motel worse than this one the first night," she said, glancing around at the no-frills decor. "And the next night one even worse than the first—in the middle of nowhere on the way to someplace I'd never heard of."

"No hunches you might be making a mistake?"

She shook her head. "It was Romance with a capital R, the kind I would tell my children and grandchildren about one day. Love at first dance. I was all over it. I was all in."

Knox rubbed at his chest, the sudden ache there. "Then what happened?"

"The third morning I woke up to find he was gone. He'd taken my stash of money, siphoned my gas, and left me a note on a fast food bag that said his declaration of love and interest in marriage had been hasty."

Knox's brows rose. "Those words?"

"All right, no." Her gaze cut from his again. "It read, 'Sorry, sweet thing.'" Her voice lowered. "And that's how I felt. Like a thing. Easily discarded. Left behind without a second thought."

He hated the pensive expression on her face but tamped down his rage on her behalf. "Should we go back to his room?" he asked, keeping his tone mild. "Shake him down for the money he took from you?"

She seemed to consider it.

"No," she said. "When I think about it, the

amount is far less than a divorce could have cost me."

"Okay," Knox said. "We could plan some sort of retribution, then. As a man from a family of seven brothers, I have no end of ideas." Tearing the asshole limb from limb came to mind.

That seemed to perk her up, and she set her beer on the bedside table. "Such as? Would we use eggs? Toilet paper?" She jumped to her feet and began pacing the room. "Am I bad for enjoying that idea so much?"

As she passed by, he set his own beer aside with one hand and reached for her with the other, tumbling her into his lap. She landed with a little gasp, and he pressed his mouth to the side of her head and breathed in her fragrant hair. "What if I told you I like you bad?" he murmured against her ear.

She shivered, and he felt her body's temperature rise, the heat transferring to the cotton and denim covering her and then to him. He stripped off his unfastened shirt, then shifted her so she sat deeper in the cradle of his body. The ends of her hair tickled his bare skin.

Erin's hands landed on the forearm that he had banded about her waist. The restless movement of her fingers ruffled the covering of dark hair, and his flesh prickled, his cock pulsed, and lust surged in his blood.

He pressed a hot kiss to her temple, then her cheek. Grasping her chin, he turned her mouth to his. "What if I mentioned that good sex is the best revenge?" he said against her lips.

She hesitated, even as her hand reached up to cup his cheek. "Knox…"

"Erin." He turned his face to kiss the heart of her palm, then gave it a quick lick with the tip of his tongue. Her body shuddered. "I'll make it good for you," he promised.

"What if I can't make it good for you?" she whispered. "It's been…so long."

His breath caught, his chest expanding with the knowledge of what she implied. "Six years? That long?"

She ducked her head. "I've, um, been reluctant. So now it's possible I've forgotten how to please a man."

He laughed, surprising himself with the soft sound when he was so damn hard and when a new, urgent need was clawing at him. It was imperative to obliterate her memories of the asshole's hands on her by replacing them with Knox's hands. Knox's touch. Knox's kisses.

He wanted to imprint himself on her. Saturate her in his scent. Make her remember no one in her body but him.

Startled by the primitive thoughts, he pushed them away and focused on her instead, lifting her chin to gaze into her anxious eyes. "What if I can guarantee it can be good for both of us? I have a surefire system."

"What's that?"

He pressed a kiss to her mouth, then drew his tongue along her bottom lip, taking pleasure in her breathy moan. "You answer all my questions."

Her eyelashes drifted down as his tongue made another pass. "What kind of questions?"

His next kiss was slow and deep, and she opened for him, wiggling closer to his body. He lifted his head. "Do you like that?"

She blinked drowsy eyes. "What?"

He smiled and nudged her cheek with his nose. "Did you like that kiss?"

"Yes."

"Good." His fingers flipped open the buttons of her shirt until he could insert his hand inside. Through her sheer bra, he found the taut peak of her breast and toyed with it, tugging until it was an even tighter bud. "Do you like me to play with your nipple?"

She squirmed and shoved her face in to his neck. "Knox…"

"This is part of my system," he said, his expression perfectly sober. "I can only promise mutual satisfaction if you do your part."

"Fine then," she said, with a trace of annoyance. "I like you to play."

"And the rest, darlin'." He promised himself patience. "You have to say, 'With my nipple.'"

She stalled.

Stilling his teasing fingers, he waited.

"With my nipple," she finally echoed, and her body quivered, so delicious.

He rewarded her by playing again with the tender bud, then nibbled on her bottom lip. "If you like my tongue in your mouth, you need to say so."

"I love your tongue in my mouth," she said, eager now. Fervent.

He laughed, kissed her lavishly, then went back to touching her, undressing her, making her tell him she liked what he was doing to her by using words she'd probably never uttered aloud to a man.

It was a fun game. Sexy. One designed to keep his six-year celibate and slightly unsure partner just a little more off-balance and a lot more aroused.

She was naked, still on his lap, and he positioned

her back to his front and spread open her thighs with his denim-covered knees. "Oh, Knox," she murmured, eyes closing, her face flushed. "We should turn out the lights."

And miss the way his big hands looked, one tweaking her nipple while the other inched down her taut belly? He didn't think so.

"What do you call this?" he asked, placing his palm over her mons so his fingers rested on the seam of her lower lips. Her hips twitched, an invitation, but he resisted, knowing she'd go wetter the longer he waited. "Erin? What do you call this?" He pinched her nipple to get her attention.

She moaned and arched her back, clearly relishing the tiny bit of pain. "I call it…um…" Her breath came in shallow pants as he released and pinched again. "Down there?"

"So unspecified," he chided. "Tell me you like me playing with all these soft, wet layers."

"Knox…" She squirmed, her perfect ass pressing against his cock, and then her hips began to rock into his exploring fingers.

He swallowed his groan. "Tell me you like me inside you." One finger. Two. Her inner muscles clenched on them, and he was the one shuddering now. "Tell me you like me touching this little button."

This time he couldn't hold back his groan as she pressed up, into his touch. "Oh, darlin'."

Still fondling her nipple with his other hand, he caressed her clitoris with two fingers, circling the hard and swollen nub. Her muscles tensed, her body strung tight, and now he switched from demand to praise, whispering how sexy she was, how desperate he was to watch her climax.

She moaned, her head turning to press her cheek to his chest as her back arched. Yeah. Now.

"Give it to me, baby," he said, and then simultaneously pinched her nipple and her clit.

She gasped, her body jerked once, then spasms rolled through her, a sweet, unmistakable orgasm. Her head turned tighter into his chest, and as she poured into his hand, her teeth latched onto his skin.

He grunted, the bite unleashing his control.

Game over.

The instant her body began to quiet, he had her up and out of the chair. His strides ate the ground, and then he tossed her onto the bed. Denim hit the floor. He was reaching for her when he remembered condoms.

Cursing even a moment's delay, he bee-lined to his kit on the bathroom counter. Then he tore back into the bedroom, as if she might disappear into thin air, to find she'd loosened the covers to stretch her perfect body on the white sheets.

Pulse pounding, he stared at her, arrested by something other than craven lust. She was so... He felt so... Rubbing at his chest, he tried to find the right words. And even though his cock was clamoring for attention, he decided he couldn't go to her until he figured out exactly what was going on. What power she wielded. Why this felt so damn important.

But then she held out her hand to him, and he was powerless to resist her.

When their flesh touched, Knox groaned, as if those answers he sought before had been found. He gave himself up to the experience, wallowing in the feel of her skin, in her sighs, in how easy it was to bring her up again.

He suckled her breasts leisurely, even as her nails dug into his scalp.

His tongue savored her taste, tickling along her ribs and then lapping at the edges of her navel.

She moved like a flower seeking the sun, bending in graceful curves as he sought new parts of her to explore—the underside of her arm, the cove behind her knee, the vulnerable line between her inner thigh and her sex.

But before he'd taken his fill of her, she was urging him up with insistent hands and entreaties. Giving in again, he covered her. She widened her legs, inviting his thrust, and he gritted his teeth and took it as slowly as he could, the intrusion into her molten heat sweet agony.

She closed over him, a tight fist of ecstasy and he rocked into her body, short lunges that sent hot chills down his spine. "Erin," he gasped out. "You make me mad."

Her answering moan sent his hand down between their bodies. He speared his fingers around the base of his cock, spreading her petaled layers so that her clit was better exposed to the rocking motion of his body. She ground upward against him and he closed his eyes, pushing deeper into her.

It was so damn good.

It had to last forever.

Which it didn't. Finally, when he thought he couldn't hold out another millisecond, her body began to stiffen. *Thank God*, he thought, burying his face in her throat.

Her muscles began to milk his cock, just the smallest of tremors, tiny ripples. Knox reached between them again and found that stiff nub at the top of her sex. Breathing hard, he rubbed it with the edge of his thumb.

She gasped and then shook, her arms and legs clasping him like a lifeline. He shoved deeper into her body, once, twice, and then felt heat sear down his spine and circle his balls before it shot up his dick, and he came in fiery bursts.

The world stopped turning.

When it moved again, he rolled off her. On unsteady legs, he made it to the bathroom to ditch the condom. Then he wet a cloth, washed himself, and wet another, making sure the temperature was warm but not too hot.

Through sleepy eyes, Erin watched him return. Instead of heading straight for her, he detoured to turn off the lights. Now the only illumination was the low glow slanting from the half-open bathroom door.

All the better to conceal himself, he thought, afraid of what his expression might reveal. Sex wasn't supposed to leave a man troubled. Though his body was sated, his mind—no longer preoccupied by the drive toward orgasm—wouldn't stop turning over the puzzle that was this tender-protective-possessive trio of braided emotions that Erin provoked in him.

He liked women. He liked sex.

He did not like feeling like this.

Sitting on the mattress beside her, he drew back the sheet she'd pulled over her breasts. Her fingers scrambled for it, missed.

"What are you going to do?" she asked in alarm, her gaze jumping to the cloth in his hand.

"Wash you," he said, nudging one silken thigh from the other. "Make you more comfortable."

"I can do that myself." She sat up and reached for

the cloth.

With a gentle shove, he pushed her back to the pillows. "Let me." It was imperative that it be his hand that accomplished the intimate task.

Her eyes wary, she stared at him.

"Let me," he whispered, opening her legs wider. *Let me. Let me.* The words coursed through him. *Let me touch you. Let me know your body. Let me care for it, care for you.*

He pressed the folded fabric to her sex, over the petals still flowered open and swollen. She flinched at the contact, and he caressed her hip with his free hand. "Sore, baby?"

"Sensitive."

He murmured a soothing sound and refolded the cloth to reveal a still-warm side that he placed against her pretty pink flesh. This time she sighed, and he held it there until the fabric cooled.

She'd relaxed fully now, her eyes at half-mast.

"A glass of water?" he asked, rising to get rid of the washcloth.

"No." Her head snuggled into the pillows as her lashes drifted onto her cheeks. "I have everything I need."

Upon returning from the bathroom, he found Erin curled up and fast asleep. That weird feeling surged again, dizzying him a little, and he dropped to the mattress, needing to be close to her again. As he arranged himself around her, his cheek settled against a cool swathe of her hair and one of his hands curled around her breast. An unfamiliar contentment washed through him—one deeper, warmer than the usual sexual afterglow—just another perplexing feeling to join the others.

Erin made a sleepy, enquiring sound.

"What?" he said, and dropped a kiss to her bare shoulder.

"Was that good sex?" she mumbled.

"Baby." Maybe after the experience she felt stripped raw, too. He gathered her closer, kissed her again to reassure her. "That was great sex."

In response, she pushed back into his embrace, her ass snugged against his groin. Her sigh seemed to move through his chest, turning over his heart.

Oh, shit, Knox thought, as the truth suddenly hit him like a pole to the forehead. This finally made sense...all of it.

Great sex, yeah.

And a huge, cosmic joke.

Because the truth was, he'd fallen in love.

He'd fallen in love with Erin Cassidy.

And while three of his brothers had taken the plunge, unserious, fun-junkie, only-in-it-for-the-grins Knox Brannigan didn't have the first idea how to deal with it.

Hours later, Knox had yet to find sleep or any answers to his predicament. He rolled from the warm bed and the even warmer Erin—refusing to look back in case he found he couldn't leave her—to slip outside. The four o'clock morning air, briny from the nearby ocean and bracing thanks to the a.m. chill, slapped him further awake.

Scrubbing his hands over his face, the sandpaper sound of his whiskers loud in the pre-dawn quiet, he sat down on the curb of the motel walkway outside his room's door. He gazed, unfocused, into the parking lot, the vehicles glazed with moisture. Then his vision narrowed on an old, run-down pick-up in the second row. It likely belonged to the asshole in 105, he decided, and wondered where he could find a baseball bat. The windshield would shatter with one satisfying *crack*.

Or maybe he'd track down a knife—even a screwdriver would do—and he'd sink it into the rubber tires just before breaking down the other man's door to shake him from sleep so he could punch him in his ugly, lying-and-leaving face. Thinking how enjoyable that would be, Knox half-rose, then sank back down again with a groan.

What the hell was the matter with him? Was this what "in love" would drive a man to? He'd had to get forceful a time or three when handling drunks at The Wake, but he hadn't been compelled to hit anyone since he was twelve and found his youngest brother Finn had taken apart Knox's favorite model airplane just so he could put it together again himself.

Finn. God, he wished he could reach his brother right this damn minute. Maybe hearing his voice would help Knox get his feet back under him. But the other man was impossible to reach on a whim given that he was currently flying off that carrier somewhere.

So without Brannigan Number Seven to connect with, he reached for his phone to call the other brother to whom he was closest.

Luke picked up with something like a low growl. "Do you know what time it is?"

"Yeah, yeah, yeah. I thought you rock climbers rose in the dark to film the dawn breaking over mountain peaks from a portaledge tent—"

"I'm in my real, very soft, very comfortable bed

at the resort. And you woke up Lizzie."

Knox winced. "Whoops. Tell her I'm sorry. I'm not yet used to thinking of you as part of a couple."

The rustling of sheets and a soft murmur told him that Luke was getting up and likely leaving the room. "All right," the other man finally said in a louder voice. "I'm heading for coffee. This better be good."

"It's not good." Knox scrubbed his free hand over his face again. "I'm in a little trouble. Or maybe it's more dire than that."

He sensed Luke's new alertness. "Trouble? You? My easygoing little brother? What's happened?"

Where to start? Knox pinched the bridge of his nose. "The yoga instructor…"

"Oh, God." Luke sighed. "What's gotten into you? You never make a misstep when it comes to women. Did you not let this one down as easy as all the others? The ones who bake you batches of cookies when you break up with them."

Knox frowned. "That makes it sound like they're grateful when we go our separate ways."

"They're happy to still be friends with you, even though you've dashed their hopes."

"That's not the case this time." *Not yet.* "You see…"

"Are you being run out of town? Do I need to wire bail money?"

"You need to tell me what to do," Knox said. "I think…I think I'm coming to care about Erin. A lot. Too much."

Luke went quiet.

"Well?" Knox demanded. "Aren't you going to say something?"

"I'm taking time to enjoy the moment I first heard

that the mighty has fallen."

"Shut up—"

"I'm doing it for all those ladies you walked away from without a scratch to your heart or your ego."

"It wasn't that many," Knox muttered. "Now get on with telling me how to handle this."

"I'm not exactly understanding the problem."

"What the hell do I know about this—this 'care' thing? It's not like I've been mooning after a Lizzie for the last decade. It's new for me." He hauled in a breath. "How do I know it won't all blow up in my face?"

"My Liz would say you have to trust and believe in the other person."

"But that's the crux of the damn problem." Impatient, Knox forked his free hand through his hair. "I've known Erin for less than a week. Mere days. But she's already made me crazy."

"Love at first sight," Luke murmured.

"I don't know. Maybe at first conversation." And the idea of that didn't make Knox any happier. "How can I go forward without a guarantee?"

"I suppose in this case," Luke said slowly, "you have to believe in yourself. Trust your own judgment."

Colin's voice boomed in Knox's head. *You never take anything seriously!* "Fuck," he said under his breath. "How can I possibly do that?"

"You have good instincts, Knox. Don't doubt it."

"Yeah?" he said dully.

"I talked to Eban," Luke offered.

Knox stiffened. "What?"

"After you and I last spoke. I was still concerned." Luke pulled in an audible breath. "He told me you're a silent partner in the bar. And he hinted you've invested in some other successful businesses."

"Damn. Why'd he do that?"

"I think to assure me you won't ride that Indian off the face of the earth. That you have responsibilities you'd never shirk."

Knox sighed. *So goes the beach bum image.*

"We should talk," Luke began, "about why you didn't want anyone to know—"

"No, we shouldn't talk about that. I'm done here. I need my own cup of caffeine."

"Fine. But you need to listen to one final piece of my hard-earned wisdom."

"Do I have a choice?" Knox asked with ill grace.

Luke sounded amused. "Not when *you* called *me* in the middle of the night."

Knox let his head drop back. "Fine."

"I've always wanted to live life in a big way," his brother said. "I know now that includes grabbing love when you find it."

Before first light, from the chair in the motel room's corner, Knox saw Erin stir. Knowing her schedule at the studio meant rising early, he'd run out for coffee for him and herbal tea for her. Her cup sat steaming on the bedside table.

Her eyes blinked, and then she rose on her elbows to look around with some confusion.

"Morning," he said, his voice soft so as not to startle her.

Her gaze swiveled his way, and she sat up higher, holding the sheet to her breasts. "Morning."

"Tea for you." He nodded toward the cup.

She reached for it, and he ran his gaze over her, enjoying—too much?—the sight of her, disheveled and rosy from sleep. The call to his brother hadn't cleared his head. Nor his chest, because it felt too full just looking on her as she pursed her lips to blow across the surface of her drink. When the covers fell to her waist, his cock surged, and he jumped to his feet, turning away before he leaped to join her on the bed.

"I have bagels," he said. "And a banana. I bought them at the convenience store."

"I need to get home. The seniors have class this morning."

He nodded without looking at her. When he finally turned around, she'd found her clothes that he'd folded on the end of the bed, and was dressed.

Her hair curtained her face as she bent over to slip on her boots.

Without thinking, he crossed to her, the distance too difficult to maintain. As he sat on the mattress beside her, she turned to him. "Knox?"

Cupping her cheek in one hand, he studied her face. "Are you all right?"

Her skin heated beneath his touch and she smiled. "You know I have no complaints."

"Good." He touched his forehead to hers and felt that heaviness swell in his chest again. "A busy day ahead?"

She shrugged one shoulder. "Classes in the morning. I do business-y stuff in the afternoon."

Should he make later plans with her? But that didn't seem smart, not when he had yet to figure out how to handle this, how to handle her.

When she stirred, he let her go, watching as she

gathered her purse and jacket. Then her gaze landed on the chair where they'd begun their carnal activities the night before, and he saw her body still.

Memories rose in his mind, teased his libido, goaded him to come up behind her. He put his hands on her shoulders and bent his head to nuzzle her hair aside in order to kiss her neck. A delicate shiver worked down her back.

He wanted to chase it with his tongue. "Erin," he whispered with raspy need.

"I really have to go," she said, her voice full of regret.

"Okay." With a last kiss, he lifted his hands, then followed her to the door.

The parking lot remained quiet as he walked her to her car. In the street, a white delivery truck rumbled by, and he watched it idly, Erin's hand in his. It was hell to let her get away from him, and every possessive urge inside him was clamoring to scoop her up and take her back to his bed.

Surely he could find some chains.

And then he had to laugh at himself because he'd become that caveman again.

"What is it?" Erin said, but her gaze remained on the delivery truck so Knox looked at it again too, and saw that it had pulled into Mickey's. Though the business was not yet open, the neon sign remained on, and an orange glow illuminated the office door.

"There's a bell," Erin murmured. "It rings in the house and Dad will come out for any after-hours or before-hours deliveries."

Was she nervous about being seen by her father? Knox shifted to block her from view, but she went on tiptoe to peer over his shoulder.

"There are several boxes," she said, then cleared her throat. "One of them could be the part for your motorcycle."

Knox froze. And if one was, indeed, the item needed to repair the Indian, he could be on his way before the end of the day, leaving behind all this confusion and unease. The risk inherent in falling in love. Before his ego or his heart might suffer any real—or at least lasting—damage, he'd be gone.

"Erin," he said, looking down at her. "I..." And then he heard his own voice in his head, an echo of words he'd once said to her. *I don't suppose you do one-night stands.*

If he left today, that's exactly all they would have.

Every trace of glibness gone, not a single scrap of charm left in his arsenal, Knox stared into her silver eyes, once more undone. His eyes closed, and that fullness in his chest began to ache.

"Knox," she whispered. One of her small hands clasped his, and she shook it a little. "Knox, look at me."

He opened his eyes, and the sky had lightened enough that he could see more of her small face, the lips still swollen from his kisses, the abrasion on her jaw where his late-night whiskers had scratched her. Lifting his thumb to it, he ghosted a touch there. "Ouch," he whispered.

"You didn't hurt me," she said, taking hold of that hand too. "I'm fine. I'm going to *be* fine if this ends today. Don't regret—"

"I don't," he hastened to say. "But—"

"I don't regret it, either." Her smile, warm and impish, did nothing to alleviate this new misery.

"Erin…"

"My choice, Knox. When I came to you last night, temporary was all I was looking for—even one night was enough."

But what if one night wasn't enough for him?

Chapter 8

—➤➤❦❦❦←—

With morning classes over, Erin showered and changed into jeans and a sweatshirt. After a quick lunch, she puttered about her kitchen, reluctant to delve into the paperwork that even a small business generated. When Marissa called, she was happy to put it off a bit longer.

"Hi," she said to her friend. "What's up?"

"I'm the DMAC, don't you remember?"

Puzzled, Erin tried unpacking the acronym. "Direct…Mouthpiece of Allergic Conditions?"

"I'm the spokesperson for hay fever?" Rissa said. "Does that even make sense?"

"No, but neither do you."

"Designated Morning-After Caller," her friend explained in a patient tone. "I phone, you give the deets about your night in the sheets. I will then pass on said deets to our other best friend at the earliest opportunity. So…how was hot and hunky Knox

Brannigan?"

Hot and hunky, that says it all. Erin cleared her throat. "Deanne figured out I was going to him."

"Of course Deanne figured that out! Now spill."

Where to begin? She didn't want to share too much because she didn't want to make too much of it. After all, it might very well be a one-and-done. "What are you doing right now?" she asked, stalling.

"I planned to pre-wash all the baby clothes and put them away today, but I didn't feel up to it. My ankles are like an elephant's and my back hurts, so I'm sitting on a stool by the kitchen sink and washing the salt and pepper shakers by hand instead."

Marissa's husband's grandmother had passed down her extensive collection of whimsical shakers to the younger woman. Unfortunately, Marissa had never liked them, and she swore she'd manage to "accidentally" break each and every one if it was her last action on Earth.

Concerned that the pregnant woman might do something today she'd later regret, Erin cleared her throat again. "Um, Rissa, you're being careful, right? You know how I adore that turtle pair, with the one little guy standing up and the other on his back with his tiny legs in the air?"

"Washed and dried."

"And the fire hydrant and the puppy? You know that's Tom's grammy's favorite. She'd hate anything to happen to those two."

"I'm looking at them right now," Marissa said, with a strange tone to her voice.

Oh, boy. Erin chewed her bottom lip. "Rissa—"

"And the frog bride-and-groom set are here, too. They look so happy." An audible sniff followed. "So cute and so happy."

Alarm filled Erin. The nicest thing her friend had ever said about any of the shakers was that they were despicably kitschy. "Um…"

"And you should see what Grammy brought me yesterday. It looks like a cracked egg and there's a baby chick peeking out. The top half of the shell sits on his head like a hat and the salt comes out of that part. Then you take the little guy out of the other half and the pepper comes from the bottom shell." Throughout this description, Marissa's voice thickened. "Do you get it?"

"Um, I think I do, Rissa. Now, take a breath—"

"It's a chick about to hatch!" the expectant mother said, on a stifled sob. "Just like my b-baby. And—"

"It was the best sex of my life," Erin interrupted hastily, trying to distract her friend from what sounded like a cloud of hormonal tears about to break. "The best sex of anyone's life, I swear. Better than a fantasy. Better than those books Deanne passed to us."

A beat of silence followed. Then Marissa whispered, "Better than a fantasy?"

"Because it was real. A real man's mouth, his fingers, his, well, his tongue and the other…parts that he knows how to use." His voice, murmuring things in her ear. The words he'd made her say that had made her blush and made her burn.

"Was it raunchy?" The other woman's tears had evaporated. "Since I turned six months pregnant, I only fantasize about raunchy stuff."

Erin laughed. "You're going to wish you hadn't told me that. Wait. *I* wish you hadn't told me that."

"Just answer the question," Marissa demanded,

sounding cross.

Yes, raunchy. *Give it to me, baby.* Her face heated. "Let's leave it that he treated me just right." Raunchy, but tender too, she thought, remembering his fleeting touch to the whisker burn on her jaw. "Just very, very right."

"Oh, Erin." Her friend sighed. "Is that man going to break your heart?"

"No," Erin replied instantly. "I'm not going to let him get that close."

And for all she knew, she wouldn't see him again, right? She was okay with that, she told herself. Totally okay.

But fifteen minutes later, when she heard the roar of a motorcycle turn into her drive, her heart jolted. "He's only come to say goodbye," she murmured to herself. "That's polite. And I'll be just as polite when I wish him good travels."

She heard him on the steps to the house's second floor entrance, the thump of his boots sounding as if he was taking them two at a time.

Eager to see her or eager to be on his way?

In any case, she waited until she heard his knock before heading to the door. When she opened it, they both froze. Knox appeared as he had the first night they'd met at the café—heavy black boots, dark jeans, his leather jacket over a dark T-shirt. Bad boy, she'd thought then, and nothing had changed her opinion, despite the gentle aftercare of the night before.

A charming bad boy, sure, but she couldn't miss the edge of danger that came with his good looks and the stark hunger in his gaze as he took her in from head to toes.

Erin locked her knees in order not to squirm and

tightly gripped the door jamb. "Well, this is unexpected," she said in a bright voice. "A goodbye stop on your way out of town?"

His brows lowered as if her reference to "goodbye stop" displeased him. "No. I…" He shoved his hand through his hair. "The Indian won't be ready until tomorrow."

She played it cool. "So the part was delivered?"

"Yeah, the coil, and your dad must have magic in his dialing finger if he could find a supplier to deliver it this fast." He hesitated. "But Cass let me borrow a motorcycle for the day—and he thought I might persuade you to go for a ride with me."

Erin couldn't hide her surprise. "My dad?"

"Apparently he thinks you don't get out enough." Knox grinned a little. "Or maybe he wanted to get rid of me. It's possible I was hovering while he worked."

Now her *dad* was encouraging her to get out of the yoga studio, just like her friends? Did everyone think she was a dull loser?

"Hey," Knox said now. "That pretty face doesn't need a frown. It needs some fun. Come with me?"

It was for her dad, she told herself, as she found herself climbing onto the back of the bike. She knew he worried about her, especially when he'd been making noises about closing down Mickey's or selling the business to his assistant, Jolly, in order to retire. He'd been investigating Mexico, hoping the warmer climate would ease the slowly increasing pain of his arthritis.

Then Knox started the bike, and she was obliged to tighten her arms around his lean waist as they turned onto the highway. The controlled speed and the cool wind made her feel like she was flying. Erin smiled to herself and settled deeper onto the leather seat. It had been ages since she'd taken a ride with her dad and, just like yoga, she realized, it could calm her mind and relieve her of cares.

No need to fret over Cass's retirement or whether to expand her yoga classes to the resort or that she might never see Knox again once he returned her home.

They rode north and east into rolling mountains covered by winter-green grasses and studded with gnarled, long-armed oaks. She lifted her face toward the stark blue sky and let the beauty and peace of the moment wash over her just like the sunshine. Smiling wider, she pulled more clean air into her lungs and sent a silent thanks to the man whose warm, strong body was in front of hers. As if Knox sensed her thoughts, he placed one palm over her clasped hands at his belly, squeezing. She hitched closer, moving her hips nearer his backside, and he squeezed again.

Possibly she sensed a swallowed groan as well.

Only something more to grin about.

Later, they stopped at a tavern tucked beneath a stand of more oaks. A popular spot, judging by the many motorcycles parked, backsides-in, along the rail of the open-air deck that circled the place. A few people gathered at the outside tables, but she and Knox headed into the building where he bought them each a beer and they found seats at a small table by a window.

Erin took a look at the clientele. Not the type to take her yoga class, she surmised, at least not in their leather and fringe, club patches and colored bandannas.

Cass would find himself right at home here.

Which made her wonder…

She cocked a brow at Knox. "Did Dad tell you about this place?"

"He mentioned it. Why?"

Glancing at the stack of bar mats on the table, the name of the bar finally sank in. *The Stagecoach Stop*—it had actually been one, once upon a time, or so her father had said. "This is where my mom and dad met." She looked around again, as if she might find evidence of the occasion. Or of her mother, Suzie Cassidy, who had neglected to send a birthday greeting to her daughter this year.

"You okay?"

She shrugged and pasted on a smile. "Sure."

"You remember much about your mom?" he asked.

"No." Scrunching up her eyes, she tried grasping the tail of any elusive memory that flitted through her mind. "The sound of a distant laugh, maybe. Her lips on my hair for a goodnight kiss. You?"

He smiled a little. "I remember leaning against my mom as she talked to a friend. Her arm curled around me, pulling me in closer. And…"

"And?"

With his fingertip, Knox traced the scars etched into the worn tabletop. "I don't eat ice cream."

Erin's eyes widened. "Oh?"

"When I was six, she went out for it one night and was killed by a new driver. I never had a taste for it after that." A moment passed, then he cleared his throat. "So, how did Cass handle becoming a single man again? He didn't remarry."

"No. And he doesn't talk much about my mom."

Knox picked up his beer and watched Erin over

the rim of his glass. "After my mother died, my dad didn't talk about her—and he didn't talk to his sons much, either. Dove into his media empire to make more piles of money and let us raise ourselves."

"Maybe it's good that working for him was a bust then."

"Because...?"

"Was he a happy workaholic?"

Knox shrugged. "I don't think so."

"If you'd stayed, maybe you would have turned out like him and lost your chance for a more satisfying life."

"I do like happy," Knox admitted. "And I don't mind work...but on my own terms."

"Not to mention men like your father make lousy husbands."

He sent her a swift glance, and Erin felt heat rush over her face. "That's right. You're not interested in marriage," she said, desperate for him to know she wasn't hinting or hoping. God, that would be embarrassing. He'd think she was like the twenty-one-year-old fool she'd been, falling for any guy who'd kiss her, believing in forevers.

"What makes you say I'm not interested in marriage?"

"You told me. The first night we met."

"Right." He nodded. "But I guess you never know. I have six brothers who I assumed were confirmed bachelors, and now three of them are committed."

"To an insane asylum?"

He laughed. "Now you sound cynical about matrimonial bliss."

"Not in a general sense. Deanne and Marissa are

moon-hopping happy. But for me... Now I don't know if I could throw myself into the idea of a lifetime promise. And I'm sure I really couldn't bear being left again."

Tears stung her eyes as she recalled the dark disillusionment she'd felt, waking up alone in that motel room hundreds of miles from home. All her youthful optimism had evaporated the moment she understood she'd been abandoned by someone she thought loved her.

Knox's hand reached out to cover hers.

Oh, God. Blinking rapidly, she slid her fingers from underneath his. "What a bore I'm being for a man who's interested in fun and games." He would *not* remember her as some weepy, emotional mess. "Tell me about...about your travel plans. Where are you off to tomorrow?"

She pasted on a cheerful, expectant expression and met his gaze. He was staring at her, an odd look on his face. Her stomach knotted. "Knox?"

He hauled in a breath. "I—"

Her phone buzzed. Putting up a finger to pause him, she pulled the device from her pocket and frowned at the caller's name, then put it to her ear. "Deanne? You usually don't call during work hours."

Listening to her friend, a cold panic shot through her bloodstream.

"I'm there," she said, lurching unsteadily to her feet. "As soon as I can."

Standing too, Knox caught her before she tripped over her chair's legs. "Erin?"

And something about the concern in his gaze and the firmness of his hold on her allowed her to become that weepy, emotional mess she'd decried a moment before. She moved into him, burying her face against his broad chest and clutching his sides. "Marissa's in labor," she said, her tears wetting the cotton of his shirt. "And it's too soon."

Knox found Erin's anxiety contagious as they rode back to her place. He didn't know much about pregnancy, but from the little she'd told him, her friend's baby wasn't yet fully cooked, and the doctors were trying to stop or stall the delivery process.

What that entailed, he had no idea, and, admitting to typical male squeamishness, refrained from asking for a fuller explanation.

As he turned into her driveway, he felt some relief. Erin had been asked to go to Marissa's place to pick up a few things and bring them to the hospital. She could get on that now.

When they came to a stop, she quickly hopped off the bike and went to work on her helmet. But her fingers fumbled with the latch, and he moved to brush them away to take care of it himself. "You're frozen," he said, the chill of her skin registering.

Frowning, he rubbed her hands with his own, trying to warm them. "I don't know if you're in any shape to—"

"Just hurry and help me with the helmet," she urged. "I want to get to the hospital as soon as possible."

"Deanne said nothing is likely to happen, right?" Knox returned to working on unfastening the chin strap. "That's the best-case scenario we're hoping for."

"I know, I know. But I'll feel better once I've fetched the things Marissa wants and delivered them to her."

Freed from the helmet, she shook out her hair and started jogging for the steps. "I need to grab my car key."

Uncertain of his next move, Knox loitered by the motorcycle. In minutes she was back and she threw him a glance as she headed to her car.

"Sorry to run out like this," she said. "And thank you for the motorcycle ride and the beer and...well, if I don't see you again, thank you for all the rest, too."

So this was the final goodbye? He hesitated, then the paleness of her face decided him. Striding to her, he pulled the key fob from her hand. "I'm driving. You look too upset to get behind the wheel, and it will give you a chance to call Deanne again."

She opened her mouth and he leaned down to press a quick kiss to her lips, silencing what he supposed would be a protest. "Get in the passenger seat," he said, nudging her in that direction.

"Knox..."

He kissed her again, swift and soft. "Let's go."

Deanne reported no change in the situation as they traveled to Marissa and Tom Farmers' house. Erin rushed to the front door and then went on tiptoe to grope at the top of one of the entry lights.

"I've got it," Knox said, coming up behind her to reach the key balanced on top. "Quite the security system."

"There's an alarm," she said, opening the door and heading to a nearby panel. "You need a code or the security company is alerted."

"Let me guess," Knox said, shoving his hands into his pockets as he watched her fingers on the keypad. "It's the digits of their wedding date."

The quick glance she sent him was narrow-eyed, but he thought he detected a hint of laughter in the silver slits. "You're annoying."

Anything to erase some of the worry from her beautiful face.

Then he followed her down a hallway. "What are we looking for?" he asked, peeking into doorways as they passed. "Looks like the contents of an entire baby boutique has been deposited in the laundry room."

Erin backtracked and grimaced at the pile upon pile of little clothes and small bed—crib?—linens. "Marissa planned to pre-wash all these things, but she wasn't feeling so great when I talked to her today. I should have known then…"

Knox drew a hand down Erin's shiny hair. "You couldn't have known. Now, what are we fetching?"

That got her on the move again. She gathered a book, a soft throw, knitting needles and yarn, a phone charger, and a hairbrush and put them into a canvas bag. A small satchel, apparently already packed, she handed to Knox. "The hospital bag."

He cocked a brow.

"The things she'll need if the baby does come." Erin swallowed hard, the anxious expression back in her eyes.

"Okay," Knox said, and slid an arm around her shoulders to bring her close again. He kissed the top of her hair. "What else?"

"Just a few snacks for Tom. He's hooked on pistachios." In the kitchen, Erin looked around with wide eyes. "Oh, Rissa."

"Wow," Knox said. "What's going on?"

Dishes were piled on every inch of countertop. Rows of crystal stemware too. The kitchen table was covered with little figurines. He touched a miniature ceramic piece of toast standing beside a tiny ceramic over-easy egg. "Are these salt and pepper shakers?"

"She was washing them." Erin took a last glance, then headed for a cupboard. "Apparently she got an itch to clean all these things."

Ignoring the mess, she tucked some snack items in the canvas bag and then declared herself ready to go. Once again at the car, she paused. "I could take you back to collect the motorcycle or drop you off at the motel before I hit the hospital. I'm steadier now."

He acted as if he hadn't heard the offer and returned to his place behind the wheel. "Directions?"

The waiting room in the maternity area wasn't crowded. There, they ran into Rob, the uncle-to-be, and learned that Tom was with his wife and Deanne in Marissa's room. A nurse pointed the way, and Erin hurried off, throwing a wan smile at Knox as she left.

In silence, he and the other man stared at the TV, while in the opposite corner a pair of older women paged through magazines.

"What's on?" Knox asked, indicating the flat screen. The sound was muted, and men in dark suits wandered around dimly lit rooms. A detective show?

"I have no idea," Rob said. "Just keeping my eyeballs occupied."

As the minutes ticked by, Knox debated with himself. Erin had safely made it to her friend's side, and he didn't have a real purpose here, being neither family nor anything beyond a passing acquaintance of the parents-to-be.

This was a hospital, so a taxi might be lurking at the entrance. Or there had to be a local car service that would drop him off at Erin's so he could retrieve the motorcycle. Rob would return Erin her car key.

Then tomorrow Knox could be on the Indian again, trying to resolve its mystery.

"Don't mess with her," the other man suddenly said.

Knox glanced over, to see Rob's attention still focused on the show. Was he following the storyline, regardless of the lack of sound? "Um, pardon?"

"Erin's special. Special to us. She hasn't brought a man around before, you know. She's not gone out in years."

Rubbing the back of his fingers along his jaw, Knox slowly nodded. "Yeah. I got that. We've talked. But...we're square, Erin and I. We know where we stand."

At least he knew where she stood. *Temporary was all I was looking for—even one night was enough.*

His own stance was less decisive. What he thought he felt for her...well, was it real? Lasting? Actually the L-word? And even if he believed it was...would Erin?

Much simpler than answering those questions, he thought, running his palms along the thighs of his jeans, would be to get up, get out, get on his way. Let her go about her life, pre-Knox.

The one in which she didn't trust that any man would stay. The one in which she didn't think she could believe in any man's lifetime promise.

Erin and Deanne walked into the waiting room and Knox found himself on his feet, Rob too.

"Well?" Rob asked. "Any news?"

His wife went to him, leaning against his side as his arm slid across her shoulders. "No change. They think they've got the contractions stopped but they could start up again at any time."

"Marissa's in pretty good spirits," Erin said, and as if her legs were too tired to hold her up, dropped to the small couch where Knox had been sitting. "Or she's holding it together for Tom."

She glanced up at Knox. "Do you know any good knock-knock jokes?"

"What?"

"Because Tom's are terrible, but I think they're his coping mechanism. We've been groaning instead of chuckling."

Knox sat beside her. "Give me a minute to think." The urge to touch her, to offer her the comfort that Rob was giving Deanne swamped him. But he was halfway out the door, and he'd just been warned not to mess with Erin.

"Maybe I could share one of your pick-up lines instead," she said. "That will make her smile. What have you got?"

Knox pursed his lips and put himself back at The Wake, listening to the bullshit that men tried on women. A wistfulness ran through him thinking of that comfortable, familiar place and the relaxed man he'd been behind the bar. Those were simpler, more carefree times—before he met yoga girl and found himself crowded with unfamiliar feelings and unwelcome doubts.

"Well?" she prompted.

He allowed himself to flick her cute nose with his finger. "How about this?" Clearing his throat, he gave her a comic leer. "Are you my appendix? Because I have a sudden gut feeling I should take you out."

Her eyes flared wide as she hooted. "You're a genius. It even has that medical angle." She jumped to her feet, full of energy again, then bent to buss his cheek. "Let's go, Deanne."

The two women hurried off, Knox and Rob staring after them.

The other man took his seat and stretched out his long legs. "It's really hard for them right now, with Marissa having this hiccup in what otherwise has been a healthy pregnancy."

Knox glanced over. "The three are close."

"Very. But it's not just that." Rob shoved one hand through his hair and then the other. "It's why we've held back on notifying any of our parents about what's going on. Rissa's live across the country now, but my mom and dad are local, and they're in the dark at the moment. We don't need to ratchet up the worry level."

Ominous.

"If you're keeping it so private, maybe I shouldn't be here," Knox said, uneasy. Christ, why hadn't he left? "I didn't know—"

"Erin didn't say, then?"

"No."

Rob studied the toes of his running shoes. "Our cousin's wife—my and Tom's cousin—was pregnant with her first child. She was a friend of our trio too, and four months ago she went into labor right when the doctor predicted. Thumbs-up."

"But…?" Because there was clearly a *but*.

"During delivery, she started seizing—an aneurism."

"Oh, God."

"They managed to save the baby, but my cousin lost his young wife on the very same day his child was born."

Oh, God.

"So, see," Rob continued, "we're all a little…agitated."

Before Knox could respond—and how should he respond?—Erin and Deanne were back.

"Another doctor check," Deanne said.

Erin stood just inside the waiting room, her arms wrapped around her waist. Holding herself, because she likely didn't trust that anyone else would.

Well, screw that, Knox thought, rising. His strides ate up the distance between them, and he yanked her into his arms, fitting her head underneath his chin.

"I've got you," he said. She shivered, and he tightened his hold. "Relax. I've got you."

"I don't know how to stand this," she said to his shoulder. "Marissa looks tired, and I think she's about to go to sleep—they're keeping her at least overnight—and Tom will stay in her room. She told us all to go home, but I'll go crazy there."

He directed Erin toward the couch and sat, cradling her in his lap. Comforting her, even though it reassured him as well to have her close. He laid his cheek on the top of her hair and tried for slow and steady breathing. "Just relax," he said again.

"I don't know if I can," she murmured. He could feel the tension humming in her body. "She's insisting we leave, but I won't know what to *do*."

Knox considered that. "Hmm," he said, after a moment. "I think I might have an idea."

She glanced up at him.

He kissed her nose. "Trust me."

Chapter 9

Wide-eyed, Erin looked at Knox as they pulled into the driveway of Marissa and Tom's house once again. It was dark now, but the landscape and entry lights glowed. "You want to eat Chinese take-out *here*?" They had two bags of the fragrant stuff in her lap, bought from her favorite local place, The Jade Inn.

"I thought once we took care of our appetites, we might take care of all that restless energy of yours."

Okay, she didn't think he meant they'd have sex at her friends' home, and she didn't think he meant for her mind to go in that direction, but it did. Bending her head to hide her blush, she gathered up the bags of food.

He came around the car to open her door and grab them from her. "Let me," he said, then led the way to the front door.

Still puzzled about his intentions, she let him

unlock the door with the hidden key. Crossing to the alarm panel, she punched in the code. "I don't know if we can find any space to eat in the kitchen," she said, remembering the dishes—everyday and fancy china— the glassware, and the salt and pepper shakers spread over every surface.

"That's what I thought we could take care of after egg rolls and chicken chow mein."

Oh. "That's an amazing idea." Staggered by his thoughtfulness, she continued to stare at him. "You remembered the mess. You're suggesting we can tidy things up."

"Do what looks like needs to be done, so when Marissa and Tom return home everything is back in place." He smiled at her. "Plus, I might want to play with those salt and pepper shakers just a little."

Erin's eyes stung.

"Hey," he said, coming forward with a rattle of the take-out bags. "I won't play with them if you don't want me to."

She gave a watery laugh. "My emotions are a little wonky right now."

"I get that." Knox shuffled the bags so he had both in one arm. He took her hand with his free one. "I heard about Rob and Tom's cousin's wife."

"Sylvia." Erin blinked away another round of incipient tears. "It was terrible."

"I can imagine." He led her toward the kitchen. There, he carefully made a place for a couple of plates among the novelty ceramic pieces and dished up food for each of them.

Erin found forks and they sat at the table.

"I'm hungrier than I thought," she said, after a few minutes of non-stop eating.

"Post-adrenaline rush," Knox said, nodding. "After a session of big-wave riding, I can eat a couple of cows."

"I'd like to see that."

He cocked a brow at her. "Really? The way I down the hooves is not an elegant sight."

"You're trying to make me laugh."

"Is it working?" He reached out to cup one of her cheeks with a big palm. "Because I find it really bothers me to see you cry."

She covered his hand with hers. "That's…nice."

His fingers slipped away, and he winced. "For the record, no man likes to be thought of as 'nice.'"

"I'll keep that in mind." She reapplied herself to her food. "And what I meant about wanting to 'see that' was watching you surf."

"Well, that's better," he said. "A chance to show off my impressive physique and my magnificent athletic prowess. I'm all for it."

"Making me laugh again."

His expression was all innocence. "Are you doubting my magnificent athletic prowess? And you've experienced firsthand my impressive physique."

Her mind wandered again for a moment, then she yanked it back to the present, and gazed with some bemusement at her charming dinner partner. "Knox Brannigan." She took his hand. "You're proving to be an excellent distraction."

His palm turned, and he entwined her fingers with his. "I want to be what you need."

Erin's heart lurched in her chest at the quietly spoken words. "I…" She dropped her gaze, to hide how much they affected her. He was just being nice, she reminded herself, as much as he disliked the compliment. It was important not to read too much into anything he said.

Knox stood, his hand leaving hers. "And right now you need a partner in disaster relief."

Erin made a quick detour to the laundry room to start a load of baby items with a special detergent she found on the folding counter, then they tackled the kitchen together. First they washed and hand-dried all the china and stemware and returned them to the cabinet in the dining room, Knox placing the items carefully on the higher shelves.

She put the first load of laundry in the dryer, tossed more things into the washer, then rushed back to the kitchen to find Knox stacking the everyday dishes in the dishwasher. "Okay?" he asked, glancing at her.

She nodded, not trusting her voice. Silly, how a handsome man performing such a simple task could affect her so. Wasn't there something about the sight of a man vacuuming being an aphrodisiac? But right now she felt the heat more in the center of her chest than anywhere else. Clearing her throat, she turned to the salt and pepper shakers. "These look newly cleaned, but we need to set them on the shelf over the window."

"How do we arrange them?" Knox said, coming to stand behind her. "Geographically?" With a careful hand, he shifted the jalapeno peppers next to the sombreros. "Or perhaps by biological kingdoms? Plantae," he pointed to the peppers and a pair of red apples. "Fungi," he said, indicating mushrooms, white and painted with purple dots. "And Animalia." He nudged a Mr. and Mrs. Moose toward two bumblebees in their black-and-yellow ceramic glory.

"What about these?" she asked, indicating a pair of robots, one black, one white.

"We'll let Ridiculous have its own section of the shelf."

It took twenty minutes of deliberating and bickering to get the extensive collection in place to both their satisfactions. Then he trailed her to the laundry room where she removed clothes from the dryer and replaced them with the final just-washed load.

When Knox moved to help her fold, she looked up at him. "You don't have to do that."

"I fold bar towels all the time," he said, matching the corners of a tiny terry piece decorated with pastel sea horses. "This can't be much different."

Everything felt different to Erin. Who knew that the hot guy she'd met at the Moonstone Café not long ago would morph into this handsome man, kind enough to help out some near-strangers in need? To help *her* out, by coming up with a productive way to keep her busy.

Together, they carried the stacks of laundry into the nursery. Knox whistled as she flipped on the light. "I'm guessing Tom made the furniture."

"Tom and Rob together." The dresser, crib, and changing table matched, each a honey-stained wood that had been hand-carved with fanciful creatures from prancing unicorns to sleek tigers with wings.

"They're like animals on a merry-go-round," he said, going down on his haunches to inspect more closely the face of a drawer.

"That's the idea."

"They have an amazing talent," Knox said, as if

to himself, wandering about the room to look at each piece.

"I'll say thank you on their behalf."

"Hmm…" he said, in absent acknowledgement.

Erin watched him run his hand along the beveled edge of the dresser. "What kind of place do you live in?" she asked, suddenly curious.

He glanced over. "Me?"

"Penthouse of stainless steel and glass? Mediterranean McMansion? Man cave decorated in classic Frat House?" She needed to know, so she could picture him in his natural element, instead of seeing him here, surrounded by soft colors. Or how he'd looked in the laundry room, folding a tiny shirt with his big hands.

"Two-bedroom cottage in Santa Monica," he said. "Not much to look at yet, because it started life a good long while ago as someone's beachside getaway. But I have a friend who wants to help me do the reno."

Then she could see that, a shirtless Knox wielding a sledgehammer.

"I like to get my hands dirty," he added, his voice sly.

She sent him a sharp look, and he laughed. Then he crossed to her, and pushed her hair off her face. "Are we about done here? You look beat."

The tender touch made her want to melt. "Yes," she said. "We're about done."

He was leaving tomorrow.

It was at the forefront of her mind as he drove them back to her house. Maybe it was why she invited him up for a nightcap—an attempt to put off voicing yet another goodbye.

They settled on her couch with a couple of beers. Erin turned on the gas fireplace to warm the living room and the TV to give her something to look at besides Knox. With their feet up on the coffee table, they sipped their beverages, and Knox idly flipped through the channels.

"Good God," he said, pausing on a commercial that showed a bunch of small boys exiting a minivan as a harried father stood by. "That's familiar, minus the hovering dad of course."

Erin tried to imagine having a tribe of siblings. "It had to be fun, at least some of the time."

"Oh, yeah. Always somebody you could cause trouble with…or to."

Erin's eyes drifted shut as she pictured a herd of male children chasing each other about. "Who's the oldest?"

"Perfect James," Knox said, and plucked her beer away from her slackening hold. She heard both bottles *clack* onto the tabletop and then felt an arm circle her shoulders.

"Which number are you again?"

"Sixth of the seven."

She tipped her head to the side to rest it on his shoulder. Any minute now she'd get up and send Brannigan Number Six on his way. A huge yawn nearly cracked her jaw. "I bet you were an adorable little boy," she said, her voice drowsy.

"Incorrigible little boy," Knox corrected. "But there wasn't anyone interested in reforming me after my mom died."

"She must have had a lot of patience to have seven sons."

"Patiently waiting for a girl," Knox said.

"I bet she loved her boys anyway."

"I think she did." Knox drew Erin more closely into the circle of his arm.

"Tired," she murmured, eyes still closed.

"Yeah, me too."

His heart beat steadily against her cheek. "Do you want kids?" she asked.

"Wouldn't know how to be a dad."

"If you had an instruction manual?"

His short laugh rumbled in his chest. "Maybe if I had the right woman, and she wanted kids."

"Are you going to find the right woman?" Erin mused.

"It's a question," he said, his voice drifting away.

Or maybe that was her, Erin thought, just as she lost the battle with sleep.

Sometime later, a buzzing woke her up. She opened her eyes, disoriented.

Gray light filtered through her living room windows. Dawn.

Her cheek was pillowed on a familiar tweed cushion. Sofa.

A warm body spooned hers from behind, and a heavy arm was draped over her waist. Knox.

That buzzing came again, and she saw her cell phone on the coffee table, doing a dance. She reached for it, Knox still unmoving.

The screen read Deanne's name and number. Instantly alert, Erin sat up, hearing her sofa-mate mumble behind her.

"What is it?" she demanded of her friend. "Is everything okay?"

"The baby's decided to arrive today despite all best efforts to convince him or her otherwise,"

Deanne said. "Come to the hospital if you want to pace and drink bad coffee like the rest of us."

On a muttered curse, Knox counted the deadwood cards in his hand, then threw them down on the upturned oil drum he and Erin's father were using as a card table. They sat in the warm winter sunshine outside the office of Mickey's Motorcycle Sales & Repair. It had to be over seventy degrees in the sheltered spot. "Seventeen."

The older man diligently added the number to Knox's losing gin rummy score. "Are you sure we shouldn't agree instead to a penny a point?"

"No." Knox scowled. Their deal was that the player with the highest score at the end of thirty games would pay the winner—the one with the smallest score—a dime a point. "I grew up with six brothers, and I know damn well it's as bad as cheating if you try to re-negotiate the terms once the competition has started."

Cass chuckled. "I learned that from my brother too."

"About Mickey..." Knox began, then his head lifted as a small car approached the business. Cass looked around too, but it wasn't Erin's little Fiat, and the vehicle continued past. Stifling an impatient sigh, Knox watched his competitor deal the next round of cards.

"You could call her, see how it's going," Cass suggested.

"Nah," Knox said, with a one-shouldered shrug. "I don't want to intrude. This is a special time for her with her friends." Despite the efforts to halt Marissa's labor, the call that morning had informed Erin that

Baby Farmer—they'd chosen not to learn the sex of their child ahead of time—was determined to have a birthday party as soon as possible.

"They're close, those three—more sisters than friends. Without a mom, Erin relied on those girls to get her through the things a dad doesn't know about or can't talk about."

"I saw that closeness." Knox picked up his hand and moved the cards about, organizing them into potential melds.

With his focus on the game, he didn't notice a truck approaching the business until it screeched into the lot, burning rubber. The smell was as nasty as the expression on Wylie-the-Asshole's face as he braked the vehicle a few short feet from Knox's chair. The driver's window winched down, and the cowboy threw a buff-colored business-size envelope out the opening, knocking the stock and discard piles of cards, the score sheet, and the stubby pencil from the oil drum so they scattered to the ground.

"It's all there," he spit out. "One-thousand five-hundred twenty-six dollars. And then the cost of seven gallons of gas."

Without raising a brow, Knox scooped up the envelope and lifted one hip to shove it in the back pocket of his jeans.

"Are you going to give it to her?" Asshole Wylie asked. "Or are you considering that payment for your services the other night?"

Knox didn't think. He was on his feet and then in the man's face, his hand shoved through the open window to fist in the collar of a cheap plaid cowboy shirt. Cotton ripped, and he felt no remorse. "Keep your insinuations to yourself," he said from between gritted teeth.

"Or what?" Wylie taunted.

Knox gave a vicious twist with his hand, making a noose out of the collar, and his voice turned low and lethal. "Turns out I have a hot temper when it comes to Erin."

The other man's face went red, and he sputtered.

"So get your big mouth and your thieving ways out of my sight," Knox continued. "And you won't find out the *what* I want to do to men who take advantage of idealistic young women."

More sputtering.

Cass came up behind him. "Uh, son…"

"Yeah, yeah. I won't commit murder on your property." He released his death grip on the shirt to leave Wylie choking and coughing. "Get gone," he told the other man, with a last, withering look.

The window rolled up and then the truck began to reverse. Knox gave the scarred and crumpled bumper a savage kick with the sole of his boot for good measure, then watched the vehicle bounce out of the lot and turn onto the road. More rubber burned as Wylie accelerated.

Then he flipped Knox an exaggerated bird.

"Pleasant fellow," Cass said mildly.

Trying to steady his raucous breathing, Knox side-eyed him. What had Erin's dad made of the cowboy's crack about payment for services? "We had some old business to settle."

Then, with pseudo-calm, he returned to the disrupted card game and bent to retrieve the cards spread about the asphalt. Residual anger pounded at his temples. "I don't think you'll see him again—he said he was heading out of town today. But…"

"That's my daughter's old business," Cass said. "I recall the amount stolen. That was him?"

"Yeah." Hauling in a deep breath, Knox slid the envelope from his back pocket and took a moment to thumb through the contents. Looked like the amount of missing cash plus another thirty or so for the purloined gas. The self-respect Wylie had stolen from Erin? Knox hadn't been able to think of a way to extract that from the cowboy's hide. The money would have to do.

He held it out to Cass. "Will you pass it to her?"

The older man put up his hands. "You're the one who got it back."

"I'm thinking I should be taking off," Knox said.

The altercation with Wylie had unsettled him, leaving his temper barely balanced on a fine edge. For damn sure he lost his head when it came to Erin, he thought. His brothers wouldn't recognize their laid-back, let's-keep-it-easy sibling in the man who'd wanted to strangle the ugly cowboy just minutes before. Knox didn't recognize himself.

Maybe moving on was the cure.

"You were waiting to hear about Marissa and Tom's baby."

Knox shrugged. "I barely know the couple." He glanced up at the sky, noting the angle of the sun. "I want to get some ground covered before nightfall."

Cass inserted his hands into the pockets of his coveralls. "Erin will wish she had a chance to say goodbye."

"We've exchanged those more than once already." Another wouldn't make going any easier. "Here. Take the money."

When it looked as if Cass would stubbornly resist

accepting the envelope, Knox shoved it back in his jeans. He'd stash it in the office or something. "We should settle my bill for the Indian." He swiped up the tattered score sheet. "And this too."

"Knox—" Cass began, but broke off when a little Fiat swooped into the parking lot. It had barely come to a complete stop when its driver jumped out of the car and began dancing around the lot, the full blue skirt she wore belling out like a ballerina's.

Her hair floated above her shoulders, and at her radiant smile, Knox's still-hot temper instantly simmered down. A grin spread over his face, and he called out to her. "Good news, beautiful girl?"

She pirouetted nearer, then leaped into his arms. Laughing, he held her high, her feet dangling, her hands on his shoulders. "Great news!" she said.

A new awareness prickled the back of his neck, and he glanced over to see Cass watching him closely. But then Erin cupped her palms around Knox's cheeks and drew his attention back to her glowing face.

"You are so damn gorgeous," he said, unable to help himself.

"I feel gorgeous." She pressed a kiss to his forehead. Then another. "The entire world is gorgeous."

Then she wiggled free and skipped over to her father. "Hi, Daddy!" She pecked his cheek with a loud smack.

"Hello there."

She started dancing again, her feet executing intricate movements that Knox recognized as Irish step dancing. He watched her, fascinated.

"I wasn't completely sure about you, son," Cass murmured. "But now, with that expression on your face…"

Erin frolicked close again, and this time Knox snatched her around the waist, before she could get away. "Okay, lady, enough of the teasing. What happened at the hospital?"

She threw out her arms. "We have a baby."

"I'm sure Cass and I have figured that out," he said, grinning again. "But isn't there a little more that you can tell us?"

"Marissa is fine. Tom might take a little longer to get over his shell-shock."

"I'm sure I'm on pins-and-needles to know how Deanne and Rob are faring—"

"Fabulous," she said, instantly.

"Spare us any more stalling, doll," her dad said, but he wore a smile too. "Boy, girl, which is it?"

"Okay, okay." Breaking free from Knox's hold, on the toes of one foot she made another single spin. "Elizabeth Erin, six pounds, four ounces. Early, yes. But healthy and sure to thrive."

"So you got the middle name after all?" Knox said, pleased for her.

Her smile was his reward for remembering what she'd told him the night they met. "And Elizabeth is Deanne's middle name."

"Congratulations to all, then." Knox ran a knuckle down her soft cheek. "That said, you're a bit ragged around the edges, darlin'."

"You look too closely."

"When it comes to you." Knox felt Cass's scrutiny again, but he couldn't pull his gaze from the man's daughter as a blush bloomed on her cheeks. God. *So* beautiful.

"We were worried, that's all," she said, "because

our Beth was arriving on scene early."

"Well, she's here now. That means you can rest. Or…what about the studio?"

"I called a couple of the seniors to get the word out and to put a sign on the studio door. Classes canceled for the day."

"All right." The envelope of money sat heavy in his back pocket. Was she concerned about losing income?

Before he could say anything, Erin was dancing away again. "My cell phone's in my purse. I have pictures."

Knox shared a look with Cass. "She's revved."

The older man wore a smile that held a tinge of sadness. "That's her mother in her, the dancing, the brightness. Like a star."

"Yes." Knox thought of her silver eyes. The sparks when they touched.

Erin was back, swiping the screen of her phone. "This one first," she said, presenting the device in the cup of her hands so that both he and her dad could view the image together.

Knox attempted appreciation. But it was a smushed scrap of humanity's face between a swaddled blanket and a pink beanie. "Wow. Clearly a wise sage for the ages. Definitely a future world leader. Not to mention a gold-medal Olympian."

She cast him a suspicious look.

"Laying it on too thick?" He lifted his hands. "I don't know any babies. Second-to-the-last son, remember? I don't remember any babies except for Finn who is still a puking mess in my mind." Knox flashed her a winning smile.

"Is that the naval aviator puking mess?"

He'd made her laugh, his favorite thing to do. "It's the G-forces."

She laughed again. Then she included her dad in her glance. "Shall we all go to dinner to celebrate? My treat."

Knox shook his head. "You don't have to—"

"I insist."

Well. It seemed as good a time as any to draw the envelope from his back pocket. "First I have to hand over something that belongs to you."

Her brows drew together as she took it from him. Then she lifted the flap and went still. "Knox." Big silver eyes lifted to his.

"Baby." He wished he could take back the intimate endearment the instant it left his mouth. His gaze cut to Cass, who wore an impassive mask, then he looked back at the most beautiful woman in the world. "Yeah. I had a conversation with the cowboy. Suggested he return your money. But I didn't demand interest," Knox added, hoping that might make his interference less objectionable.

"Dad," Erin said, addressing her father. "Do you know anything about this? Were you around when this money was miraculously delivered?"

The man lied like a rug. "Huh? I have no idea what you're talking about."

She inhaled a long breath and shifted to face Knox. "You're crazy, you know that?"

Crazy about you.

After a moment, she sighed, clearly torn. "I suppose I shouldn't look a gift horse in the mouth." Her fingers riffled through the bills. "All right. Then it's going to be a very nice dinner, right, Dad?"

"Oh, I can't go," Cass said, hands in his pockets

again. "Sorry, but who'll keep an eye on the dogs?"

Resigned amusement crossed her face. "*Dad...*"

"Kidding." Cass avoided Knox's gaze. "It's my poker night, remember?" Then, his head came up and turned, as if he heard something from the garage bays. "Excuse me." The older man strode off.

Erin slapped the envelope against one palm. "I can't decide if I should be mad at you or not."

"I like the second choice better."

"Okay, then. But only if you let me buy you dinner." She flashed him an expectant smile.

"Erin..." He reached out to touch her face again, but let his hand drop.

Damn it, he'd made the decision to go. No more caresses, no more kisses, no more procrastination.

She must have seen his resolve on his face.

"Oh," she said, her smile dying. The touch of disappointment in her eyes almost killed him. "You're leaving. Now?"

"Yeah." He nodded, hesitant to exchange another damn goodbye. He was so sick of saying that word to her. "Soon."

"But not sooner than tomorrow," Cass said, strolling up to them.

"What?" Knox stared at the older man.

"Jolly's found a little trouble with your points," he answered, cheerful. "It's going to take some extra work."

Knox looked from the man to his daughter. She didn't say a word. She didn't have to. Because spending more time with Erin was an irresistible temptation. Knox swallowed a curse at his own wavering determination. "It looks like you have yourself a dinner date then, darlin'—if the offer's still open."

Maybe, he thought with bleak hope, tonight he'd find a way to work her out from under his skin.

Chapter 10

Erin knew she and Knox had been saying goodbye since the moment they'd met. They'd even uttered the word more than once. But this time, she felt it to her bones. Goodbye. The end.

It was enough to pop the champagne bubbles that had been rushing through her bloodstream since Elizabeth Erin Farmer made her way into the world that afternoon.

"Are you okay?" Knox asked, his voice quiet. He caught her hand as they crossed the parking lot toward the fancy restaurant located at the spa-resort south of town.

"I'm great," she said, forcing a smile. This was supposed to be a celebration.

Reaching the door, he pulled it open and ushered her through. "You look beautiful," he said, bending to murmur in her ear as they waited for the hostess.

Erin resisted the urge to stroke the smooth knit of

her wrap dress. Midnight blue, the garment ended just above her knees and tied in front below a deep vee of a neckline. The long sleeves were of dotted mesh, the same color as the dress itself, but the hint of flesh through the sheer fabric somehow made the bare parts of her—legs, throat, the small amount of cleavage she could create with a push-up bra—seem even barer.

Glancing at Knox, she noted again that he'd dressed up too—his look halfway between gentleman and biker. Along with his dark jeans and motorcycle boots, he wore a cream-colored dress shirt topped by a fitted navy blazer. She touched one light wool sleeve. "Don't tell me you had this in the Indian's saddlebags."

He grinned, tripling handsomeness that was already off the chart. "Cass—"

"My dad has never worn anything like that in his life."

"—gave me directions to a men's store," he continued. "I couldn't embarrass you by showing up in my old Velvet Lemons concert T-shirt and my motorcycle jacket."

To her mind, iIn whatever he wore he would outshine all the other men in the place, she thought, as they were led through the restaurant, passing by the elegant bar on the way to the dining tables draped in starched white linens. The one she'd reserved was positioned along a glass wall overlooking the Pacific, a prime spot for the view as well as to see and be seen by the other well-dressed diners.

Using her connection with the spa-resort through Yoga Girl, she'd pulled strings to get the best seat in the house.

She'd wanted the night to be special.

A special "*Goodbye*," she reminded herself.

They settled into the cushioned chairs and were asked if they wanted cocktails. With an impish smile, Erin glanced at Knox.

He met her gaze, smiled too. "She'll have a mai tai," he said. "For me...what the heck, go ahead and bring us a pair of them."

A sudden clutch of concern in her belly took her mood down another notch. mai tais. The two of them had a drink now! Okay, it was a joke, but an in-joke that only they shared and it might be nearly as dangerous as having a song. More dangerous? A song could go out of fashion, eventually you wouldn't hear it on an elevator or while on hold on the phone, but a mai tai was an enduring standard.

Destined to live forever.

Like her memories of Knox Brannigan.

Erin swallowed, hard.

"Hey, hey, hey," he said, reaching across the table to grasp her hand. His was hard and warm and slightly rough.

Her belly clutched again.

"What's wrong?" Knox smoothed his thumb over her knuckles.

And before she had to lie, the server returned with their drinks and a bowl of newly roasted mixed nuts, hot and salty, a spa staple.

"Well?" Knox asked, lifting his glass. "To Elizabeth Erin Farmer?"

Erin grasped at the thought like a lifeline, and then went on to keep the conversation light by regaling Knox with stories from the waiting room at the hospital, where the Farmer grandparents, Jeff and Misty, had worn holes in the flooring and blamed each other for being banned from the labor and delivery room because of their sympathetic but very loud wincing every time Rissa had a contraction.

Knox winced now too. "Could we skip the details?"

"Such a man," she said, airily, and was about to tease him with talk of umbilical cords and breastfeeding, when a light hand touched her shoulder. Erin glanced up, then pushed back her chair to stand.

"Katie!" she said, hugging the other woman. "How are you? I haven't seen you since—"

"Our yoga certification classes." The blonde wore her hair in a long braid that she pushed over her shoulder. "Remember Kelly and I moved to Sacramento?"

"Yes, of course, and your twin is well too?"

"Fine, both of us are fine, and we've moved back to the area. My boyfriend and I were tired of the long distance thing, and it made more sense for me to return than for him to uproot his massage therapy business."

"We'll have to get together."

"I'd like that—Kelly and I both would. We'll pick your brain for what's new in the area and how we can make some cash. We're only going to work part-time with my boyfriend, and we don't want to leave yoga behind."

"I have a studio now," Erin said. "Two years old."

"Oh! We could take some classes with you."

"Sure…" Erin glanced over at Knox, then realized how rude she'd been. "I'm sorry, Katie, this is Knox Brannigan. Knox, Katie Richards, from—"

"Yoga certification," he said, standing to shake the other woman's hand. "I heard. Nice to meet you."

Katie gave the man a once-over then looked back at Erin, a *wowza* expression on her face. "You've been busy."

"With the studio," Erin said firmly. But a new idea flashed in her head, one brought on by the person she'd called at the resort that day when she'd pulled that string for the primo table. "And about that..."

"Yes?"

"I have a contact here at the spa who's trying to interest me in putting on some classes here, maybe even some workshops and weekend retreats centered around yoga. But taking that on solo, as well as my regular schedule at the studio, would be too much for me."

Katie's eyes widened. "You'll need some help?"

"I think so." Erin glanced at Knox to see him nod. "Yes. If I go forward, I'll need additional instructors. Are you interested?"

A few minutes passed as they exchanged phone numbers. Katie thought she could speak for herself and her twin to say they were both very interested in learning more about what Erin had in mind.

"I'm not sure I know exactly *what* I have in mind," Erin admitted to Knox, after the other woman returned to her table of friends at the bar.

"But you have options now," he said, then the conversation paused as the server returned with the bottle of wine they'd selected. Next came their salads and then their matching dinner plates. They didn't return to the earlier conversation until they were sampling bites of garlic mashed potatoes, steamed green beans amandine, and swordfish steaks topped by dabs of avocado butter.

"Taking on some employees is a good move for you, Erin," he said, scooping up more potatoes.

"I don't know that I would have seriously considered it, or considered the idea of classes here at the spa, if you hadn't encouraged me."

"I like to think I have good instincts about what will work and what won't," he said. "And I also have faith in you. If growing your business is what you want, then you'll do it."

He had faith in her. The words boosted her confidence, and she smiled at him, then swung her leg to nudge his with the toe of her shoe. "You can make a woman feel pretty darn good, do you know that?"

It could have been taken in a sexual way—because he had to know he was excellent in that department, too—but he merely reached for her free hand and gave it a brief squeeze with his. "I'm glad. And I'm glad we met, Erin."

Before she could do something to embarrass herself, she nodded and gave her attention once again to her meal. A few beats of silence passed, then Knox spoke again.

"You know, if you do get some other instructors on your payroll, that could really change things for you."

"I'll have to bone up on employee workplace rights," she said, with a little grimace. "Not something I know too much about."

"You can also plan some real time off for yourself."

Erin glanced up at Knox, surprised by the thought. "Time off."

"A concept that's especially pleasant when you

can string days of time off together. In case you've forgotten, those are known as weekends, even long weekends, and, dare I mention it, vacations." He was smiling at her.

And then his expression turned serious. "Erin, that means…" He looked away, seeming to struggle with something.

"That means?" she prompted.

His gaze returned to her face. "We could see each other again. You could come visit me in Santa Monica. I could take you to my brother's resort in Yosemite. This wouldn't…"

Have to end, she finished for him. Their goodbye wouldn't have to happen after all.

The appeal of the idea was no surprise, but her fear of it was. A cold wave washed over her as she imagined herself arriving on Knox's doorstep one day for a long weekend, only to see regret in his gaze…or disinterest.

Was it wrong of her to imagine the worst that might happen? The best could be some shared days here and there, pleasant times spent catching up on their separate lives. Spent in bed.

He'd mix her mai tais at cocktail hour and she'd make him pancakes for breakfast and they'd go for motorcycle rides and walks on the beach. And then the real world would reassert itself. They'd have to part once more…if not a goodbye, but a so long until…until…

Until such casual relationships, however warm in intention—however hot in the sack, fizzled out.

A situation like that was sure to disturb her inner harmony. She'd definitely find herself out of the driver's seat of her life.

On a sigh, Erin glanced up to see the resort admin and yoga student, Lindsay Fox, approaching with a welcoming smile on her face. As she paused beside their table, Erin greeted her. "Hey, it's nice to see you."

"Just making sure your dinner is to your satisfaction," Lindsay said, then introduced herself to Knox. "I hope you're enjoying your evening."

"We are," he assured her.

Then Lindsay turned to Erin again. "Could I interrupt you just a moment to set up a couple of meetings?" She made a face. "Rude, right? But I'm so excited about our ideas!"

Hesitating, Erin glanced at Knox.

"Go ahead, ladies," he said. "Don't mind me, I'll just be sipping my wine and savoring the view."

But as Lindsay consulted her calendar app on her phone, Erin couldn't help noticing that Knox's attention was caught not by the Pacific Ocean on the other side of the glass, but by a sweet charmer at a neighboring table. A rosy-cheeked cherub—probably not yet two—sat in a stroller across the narrow aisle. She stared at him with fascinated interest. Wearing a bemused expression, Knox looked back.

The cherub ducked her head, inserted her thumb in her mouth, then glanced up at him again through the veil of curly dark lashes.

What a little flirt!

It made Knox grin, and smooth operator and ladies' man that he was, he wiggled his fingers at her. The little girl smiled around her thumb and uncurled the tiny digits hooked on her nose to wave back. Then she stretched her other hand to present Knox with a small stuffed dog.

The animal was pink and a little grubby around the edges. An ear was torn, and in the place of one black embroidered eye was a patch of yellow felt attached with crude white stitches. Clearly a well-loved toy.

Knox refused to take it by shaking his head, but Sweet Charmer's brows slammed together, and she offered it to him with more insistence.

Uh-oh, Erin thought, as he reluctantly took it out of her hand. This could go badly.

But she shouldn't have underestimated his ability to handle any female—including one pint-sized. Lifting the dog, he inspected it gravely and stroked its mangy plush from neck to tail. Then he pressed a kiss to the top of its head, and returned it to the child, with a little bow as if to thank Charmer for momentarily sharing her beloved.

The toddler beamed.

And another cold wave doused Erin. This time, it was the truth.

There could be no getaway weekends, no mai tais, and no long mornings in bed with the man across the table.

That would only court trouble for Erin. Because she was already a hair's-breadth from doing something extremely undisciplined and in the long-term dangerous to her heart's health—namely, falling in love with Knox Brannigan.

Knox trailed Erin toward the restaurant exit, his mood lowering with each step. It hadn't escaped his notice that she hadn't jumped at the idea of seeing him again once she scheduled herself some free time.

Hell. What had he been thinking to propose it,

anyway? That notion of his had been more than misguided. A long-distance romance with her would never satisfy him.

Much better to end it altogether and hope that this surprising passion died a swift and pain-free death.

Tomorrow he'd take off on the Indian and…what?

Leaving Southern California, his goal had been two-fold. One, he'd thought to re-discover his former self, the Knox Brannigan who was a player at all things, who took a casual approach to every aspect of life, including relationships with family and with the female sex.

Yet now he couldn't see himself being so cavalier ever again. In the few short days he'd been away, the absence of a closer connection with his brothers had gnawed at his soul. He couldn't let that continue. As for women—

There too, he'd probably been much too careless. He hoped fate wasn't going to punish him for it now.

In any case, he'd climb onto the motorcycle the next day and see if he could achieve his other goal— finding some understanding of why the Indian had been left to him. His brothers had gained clarity about themselves and about Colin himself since their father's death, while Knox only had more questions.

At the prospect of never having answers to them, a now-familiar dark weight settled over him again.

At the hostess desk, Erin stopped to inspect a large bowl of individually wrapped mints. Knox shoved his hands into his pockets just as cold, insect-like feet skittered across the back of his neck. He slapped a palm there and obeying some odd hunch turned, glancing around the bar area through which they'd just passed.

At the far end, striding through glass doors that led to a patio lit with twinkling lights and two fire pits, was a dark-coated figure with wide shoulders and a familiar shock of white hair.

Colin Brannigan.

Knox's air left his lungs in a rush. His belly knotted, and then he was moving, striding toward those doors only partly aware that Erin was calling his name.

Fury flashed through him. How could Colin have lied to them? How could he have deceived the seven sons who had been shocked by his "death?"

A hand plucked at his sleeve, and he kept walking, his gaze trained on the exit that he'd seen his father walk through.

"Are you all right?" Erin asked.

"I have to do this," he said, shoving through a glass door, then catching it at the last second so it wouldn't shut in Erin's face. But his gaze swept the patio and there—*there*—near the far fire pit, he spied Colin. His back to Knox, the man seemed to be chatting calmly with a party of several others, clearly unaware his seething sixth son was on his scent.

He stalked forward, his vision tunneling to that burly build and that distinctive hair of his father's as both betrayal and gladness roiled in his belly.

Erin continued to speak, but he couldn't hear her words over the thudding boom of his heart. Then he was behind Colin, close enough to touch him, and he was aware of the faces of the others seated around the flames lifting to look at him, their expressions puzzled.

Knox raised his hand to get his father's attention,

pausing when he noted how it trembled. Then a spike of fresh rage cleared away his hesitation. The man had let them believe he was *dead*.

"And you criticized me as a player," he spit out, grasping Colin's shoulder. "What kind of game is this, you son of a—"

As the man turned, Knox went speechless. He felt as if all his blood drained from his body as the other person got to his feet.

"Do I know you?" The stranger's beetle brows came together over his hawkish nose.

Not Colin's nose. Not Knox's father's face.

His mouth worked, and at first nothing came out. Then he swallowed. "Some trick of the light," he managed to choke out. Some trick of the mind. "I mistook you for someone else." Nausea filled his belly, and for a shameful second he thought he might heave on the man's polished shoes.

Erin tucked her hand in the angle of Knox's elbow. "We apologize for interrupting." Her fingers squeezed his arm. "You're sorry, right, honey?"

Her pretty features and pretty apology might help him save face.

"Yes. Sorry," Knox said. Though his muscles felt stiff, he managed to signal to a passing server. "Another round of drinks for this table on me, please."

"We'll pay for it at the bar," Erin added, with another squeeze. "Let's go, honey. The babysitter awaits."

Then she looked toward the guests at the table. "Triplets. We're a little sleep-deprived."

They left to understanding noises from the women in the group. Erin practically hauled Knox off the patio and then out of the restaurant after their brief stop to pay the tab.

He let himself be led to her car and folded into the passenger seat without a word. What was there to say?

One of her last memories of him would be of him making a fool of himself.

A lump of emotions he couldn't separate sat like a weighty ball in his belly. Letting his head fall back to the seat cushion, he closed his eyes and breathed heavily, trying to settle himself.

Then the car stopped, and Erin was tugging at his arm. "Come inside. I'll make you green tea. It will help."

He owed her for the scene he'd just put her through, so green tea would be the price. As he exited her car, she watched him with big eyes. "It's okay," she said in a kind voice, as they walked toward the stairway leading to her front door. "We'll talk."

Talk? He shook his head. "For God's sake, no."

What he needed was distraction, he decided. Action. Something to focus on besides that ugly weight inside him that seemed to be growing by the second. His gaze caught on the door to the utility closet under the stairs and he halted. An idea took hold. "That last wall," he said.

Frowning, she glanced at him. "What?"

"I have a last wall to paint in the locker rooms. I did some repair work and then primed it, but I didn't get to the final coat." He made his way to the door and stripped off his jacket to toss it on the ground.

"Not now," Erin said, following at his heels and then grabbing up his discarded garment. "This isn't the time. You're wearing nice clothes."

Instead of answering her, he flung open the door.

The automatic light flipped on, illuminating mops and brooms, a few basic tools, and the painting implements and cans on shelves attached to the rear wall. "Who put that stuff back there?" he muttered.

"The cleaning people were in," Erin said. "Come on, leave this. We'll take care of the painting another time."

"The time is now." To get to what he wanted, he began yanking out buckets and mops and jugs of cleaning supplies.

"Knox, please."

Her voice was a buzz in his ear as he continued clearing his way. His sleeve caught on a shelf and at the ripping sound he looked down and noticed a couple of tears and then dirt and grease stains all over his new dress shirt.

No matter, he thought, and carried on with the task.

Finally, he had a two-gallon can tucked in one arm with a smaller one balanced on top. In his free hand he gripped a paint tray, with a scraper and an open utility knife rattling around at the bottom.

Crossing the threshold, he encountered Erin, her hands on her hips and an expression of exasperation on her face. "You can't really mean to do this."

"I really mean to do this," he said, brushing past her.

Then his foot caught on the handle of a bucket and he tripped. The paint, the tray, and everything else tumbled from his hold as he struggled to remain upright.

"Are you okay?" Erin hurried forward as he regained his balance. "Let's go upstairs. We'll put it all away tomorrow."

"*No*." Suddenly infuriated by his own clumsiness and by that stupid moment when he'd mistaken a stranger for his father, Knox grabbed up the offending plastic bucket and threw it as far as he could, until it skittered along the asphalt where her students parked. His hand found a broom next, and he sent it sailing like a javelin in the same direction.

Erin's eyes went wide. "Knox, stop."

But stopping wasn't an option. Instead he continued hurling item after item after item across the parking area, as anger rushed like fire through his blood and a sour metallic taste rose up his throat to coat his tongue. His fingers closed around another implement, and then a sharp, bright pain made him freeze.

Erin gasped. "You're hurt."

He glanced down to see he'd seized the blade of the utility knife and that blood was dripping down his hand to his wrist. More of it was spattered on his dirty shirt.

He shifted his gaze to Erin, and at her horrified expression all his riotous emotions quieted. *Don't scare her*, he thought, locking himself down. *For God's sake, get control.*

"I'm okay," he assured her, his voice hoarse. Loosening his fingers one by one, he let the knife clatter to the ground. "It's nothing. I'm okay."

She came slowly toward him as he held his bleeding flesh to his soiled shirt. "Don't be afraid," he said, replaying the last few minutes in his head. What a beast. He hauled in a deep breath and let it out slowly. "I'm sorry. Don't be afraid."

"I'm not afraid of you. I'd never be afraid of you." Taking his uninjured hand in hers, she tried tugging him toward the stairs. "Let me look at that in the bathroom."

"Erin…"

She tugged again. "This way."

He complied, wanting to reassure her he hadn't lost his mind. It was just…he couldn't explain what had happened. For a few minutes, all the darkness surrounding him lately had taken over.

In the bathroom, he blinked under the light's glare. She left him leaning against the countertop as she collected first aid supplies. "Do we need to go to the emergency room?"

He took his hand from his belly and inspected the shallow cuts. "No, it's nothing."

Without answering, Erin ran his hand under cold water. Then she delicately dried it before smearing each injury with ointment.

He glanced from his hand to his reflection in the mirror, startled by his dishevelment—his hair mussed and his clothing filthy. No wonder she'd stared at him with such wary eyes. Beast, indeed. "Hell," he said in disgust. "I can't bear to look at myself."

Erin continued her ministrations, now applying elastic bandages. "Then why don't you try taking a look at your grief instead?" she said, her voice as gentle as her touch.

His grief? His *grief*? While his brothers had been saddened upon learning of Colin's death, he'd pretty much accepted it right away. *It is what it is.* Then later, yeah, the doldrums had come to visit, but that persistent gloom didn't mean…

Grieving? Why would he have been grieving?

"I hadn't seen him in months," he said.

Instead of answering, Erin wound another

bandage around another finger.

"I don't know that he even liked me." Knox shoved his free hand through his hair. "He certainly didn't like my attitude." *You never take anything seriously!*

"He was still your father."

Knox recalled that gladness he'd felt when he thought for a moment he'd found Colin alive. "And I'm not sure I liked him," he confessed. "He had his admirable qualities, sure, but…"

"You can grieve for what might have been, too, you know."

You can grieve for what might have been.

God. Was grief that dreary presence that had been either bottled up inside him or hanging on his back for the last couple of months?

Grief. A natural, normal response to loss.

Just the idea that what he'd been experiencing was something so…ordinary, something to be expected, seemed to lighten the darkness. Maybe acknowledgment of it was the first step to managing the condition. He inhaled a long breath, testing the thought. For weeks he'd felt like something alien had come over him. Now it had a name. And understanding that he grieved for his father made him…made him feel like a better son.

On a wave of gratitude, he stared at Erin's head, still bent over his hand. How had she known what plagued him when he'd been without a clue? "Baby," he murmured.

She looked up, and he could barely breathe as another emotion rolled through him, filling his chest and filling his head, the emotion he'd come to recognize as love.

He cupped her face with his good hand and she turned her head to kiss his palm.

"Okay now?" she asked.

"Always okay with you."

"Good." She glanced away from his face to start unfastening the buttons on his shirt. "This grubby thing has got to go."

Watching her carefully, he let her strip him of the offending garment. Then he stood half-naked before her, and his body reacted as a male body would react. Her gaze shifted lower, and he knew she noticed the heavy bulge in his pants.

"Purely biological," he said, trying to inject a proper note of apology in his voice. "Your hands on me will do it."

Silver eyes met his. "I like touching you." Her palms stroked his bare chest, then moved lower to cup him over his pants.

Knox sucked in a sharp breath. "I like touching you, too." And more of that warm euphoria surged through him as, in answer, she took up his uninjured hand and held it to her breast.

"Let's go to bed, Knox."

Chapter 11

—➤➤❮❮—

Erin wondered if she should take back the offer. He'd been through so many moods tonight, and maybe it wasn't fair to push him into something as personal, as intimate, as sex. But when a smile grew on Knox Brannigan's handsome face and he took over to guide her out of the bathroom and toward the bedroom, she saw him for the experienced man he was.

Remember how he'd soothed her nerves and boosted her arousal by that game of "Tell Me" in his motel room?

The sharing of sexual gratification came easy for him. He didn't attach undue importance upon it.

She was just another in a line of willing pleasure-partners.

Not that he was selfish at all—he gave with a generosity that communicated he deeply enjoyed a woman's body—but she supposed they might be almost generic to him.

Lips, breasts, the curves and valleys, the softness and heat, all one and the same.

And that was fine, Erin told herself. Then she would be able to stay safe behind her own private gates. He wouldn't reach any dangerous territory that would make her vulnerable to him. That could cause her pain.

Her bedroom was dimly lit by the small lamp atop her bedside table. She glanced about her room and blushed a little, thinking how it might appear to him. It wasn't a room decorated with male guests in mind. Scarves hung from the edge of the big mirror over the dresser.

An old stuffed animal sat on the chair in the corner.

Gah. It made her feel about as young as the toddler who'd flirted with him at the restaurant earlier. He caught the direction of her gaze and dropped her hand to cross to the toy. "Now what is this?" In his bandaged hand, he held up the bedraggled tan bear with its nearly shredded blue satin neck ribbon.

She tried for a semblance of dignity. "Something between a rite of passage and a badge of honor. Randy Gunderson won it for me at the autumn fair when I was thirteen years old. Deanne and Marissa were green with envy. And it really upped my standing in the seventh grade."

He smiled at the bear then tossed it back on the chair. "I recall winning a stuffed animal for Tiffany Gilbert, but it was an overgrown snake. However, it got me to second base."

Erin rolled her eyes. "I suppose that was also in seventh grade."

He merely smiled, then sauntered to her again. "I don't remember. And I don't remember much about Tiffany, really. I know she was not as pretty as you."

Erin's pulse leaped as he stroked his thumb down her neck. She was supposed to be the *same* as Tiffany! Not prettier.

Lifting her hair away, he bent to trace his tongue along the rim of her ear. Fiery chills dashed away from the wet touch to run down her neck and along her arms.

"You can be so adorably girly, Erin," he murmured. "I loved all that dancing you did this afternoon."

Her hands clutched his taut sides as her knees weakened. "Ballet. Tap. Jazz. Years of classes."

He pulled his head away to look down into her face. "What would it take to get you to show me that? Some of all of that?"

"No." She cleared her throat. "You saw me lead a yoga class, isn't that enough?"

"I had to stop watching," he admitted, a wicked gleam in his dark eyes. "I was afraid I'd get too worked up and your seniors would have me arrested for lascivious imagining."

She laughed, a little breathless. Then his mouth moved hotly on her neck. "Erin. God, what you do to me."

No. What *he* did to *her*. Afraid she was about to become a puddle at his feet, she pulled away and turned to present her back. "Can you undo the zipper?" It was nearly impossible to reach.

"I could," he said, "if you'd show me just one...what is it called? An arabesque?"

Now where the heck had Knox Brannigan learned

that term? She glanced at him over her shoulder, her eyes narrowing.

His expression turned sheepish. "The things you pick up from somewhere," he said vaguely.

"A ballet position?" He'd likely been with some professional dancer at one point in his life. "Was she a stripper?"

He laughed. "No."

"Well, I can't do anything like that in this dress without ripping stitches."

"We can't have that." He inched down the zipper, his mouth tracing each inch of bare flesh he revealed. "No one tastes like you, Erin."

His big hands brushed the dress off her, and she caught it as it fell toward her knees. Stepping out of it she glanced down at the black lace strapless bra and the cheeky little matching panties.

As a yoga practitioner and instructor, she didn't have big hang-ups about her body. But that didn't mean she wasn't curious about Knox's reaction to it in the fancy underwear. She glanced at him over her shoulder.

His skin looked stretched over the bones of his face. His hands were clenched into fists. And his gaze felt hot on her skin.

Erin had the silliest impulse to throw an arm over her breasts and a palm over the apex of her thighs. But hadn't he seen every naked inch of her before?

"Baby," he said, and there was a dark, longing note in his voice. "Come closer."

"I have to put away my dress." She approached her closet on unsteady legs. When she turned from the task of hanging the garment, it was to find him right there, his big body looming between the jambs of the door.

He reached around her and ran his hands over the clothes, making them wave on the pole. "I love this room. Everything smells like you."

The sudden ache in her chest made her push him back to put some distance between them. "You don't have to say things like that."

His frown lasted but a moment then he narrowed his gaze at her. "Second thoughts?" he asked, softly. "Always your choice, Erin."

"No second thoughts." Give up his kisses and caresses for what would be the last time in her life? Not a chance. She smiled at him and walked nearer to draw her fingertips down his hard chest. "It's just...strange to have you in my bedroom." Was her space ruined forever she wondered with a sudden clutch of worry. Would it always seem incomplete without the addition of Knox Brannigan's special brand of masculinity?

He put his hands on her waist and drew her closer for his kiss. His tongue explored the inside of her mouth until she was squirming, wishing he'd move his hands and stroke her heated skin.

She drove her fingers into the thick hair at the back of his head and held there, prolonging the deep kiss. It caused his hand to finally move too, sliding down to run over her panties.

"Very nice," he murmured against her mouth, one fingertip tracing the lower cut of the lace, which left some very sensitive skin bare. She wiggled and he squeezed the curve, drawing her against him so his hard shaft pressed into her belly.

The feel of it made her hotter, wetter. She broke from his mouth to take in great gulps of air, and he pressed his cheek against hers. His whiskers were the barest touch of sandpaper—clearly he'd shaved before their dinner out—but still the tiny scrape caused more chills to flash down her body.

"Beautiful girl," Knox whispered. He pressed a kiss to her temple, her cheek, her nose. Sweet, soft kisses that made her heart flutter. "*My* beautiful girl."

She had a moment to stiffen at the danger of the words and then he soothed her with a soft noise. "My beautiful girl for tonight."

Everything turned dreamy after that. He pulled her bedcovers down and placed her on the plumped pillows, following her to the sheets where he began stroking and tonguing her skin in long skims and light tickles that turned her feverish. Achy. Ready.

He laughed when she tried directing him with her hands and caught her wrists to hold them over her head.

Delicious capture.

There was no feminine concern at his firm but gentle hold. She didn't feel weaker or at risk, but instead pushed deeply into the pillows and arched her back in order to do her best to encourage his wandering mouth. His soft laugh was yet another caress, and then he obeyed her unspoken demand and sucked on her hardened nipple through the lace of the sheer bra.

She trusted him, she thought, as a wave of lust rippled her belly and made her arch again. Should she worry about that?

But it was impossible to think clearly when Knox's clever mouth and hands moved over her. But not merely clever, she thought in that hazy way again. Cherishing.

Cherishing.

That only aroused her more. She undulated in his hold as he drew down her strapless bra with his teeth so it banded below her breasts. Hovering over her, he stared at them, then looked up at her face.

"Everything about you is made for me," he said.

Pretty talk. Just pretty talk, she assured herself.

Then his mouth was busy at the hard peaks, taking her out of her head until she was only aching sensation and coiling tension. His lips slid down her torso, and he was using his teeth again, a tiny bite on the rim of her navel, on the soft flesh just above the elastic of her panties. They managed to drag that scrap of lace down her hips and thighs, and she wiggled and twisted until she could toss them away with one foot.

He was hovering over her again, now between her spread thighs so he could look at her there and she felt anticipation build, her pulse pounding. "Made for me," he murmured again, then bent his head to taste her.

She flew, faster than that motorcycle ride. Faster than a shooting star in the sky.

His gentle mouth stayed with her through it all, soothing her as the last contraction twitched away. But then he started licking again, her hips in his big hands, until she was panting again, aching again, needing more.

Needing him.

She urged him up, and he found a condom and then he found her, hot and wet and ready for his first thrust.

They both cried out.

He was moving, a sure but slow rhythm, as he pressed kisses on her throat, her jaw, her mouth. Her hands clutched at his hard shoulders, her anchor in the heat and the building bliss.

She moaned, seeming to snap his control, and his breathing turned ragged as the movements of his hips sped up. Wanting to hold all that masculine power in her hands, Erin's palms slid down his back to his rounded buttocks and the hard, bunched muscles there.

Knox groaned. "Erin...God." He moved with more urgency, and her own pleasure rose in sharp staggers with each deep lunge.

Then he insinuated his hand between them, touching her on the slippery peak of her sex, nudging her that last distance until she took off again.

Her climax triggered his and he shivered hard and shook on another long groan. Then he collapsed over her, his head on the pillow his face turned in to her throat. His breathing calmed, and he gave a lazy lick to her tender skin. Then another.

It was her turn to shiver.

"I love you, Erin," he whispered, each syllable a puff of warm air on her damp skin. "I love you."

Oh, God. With his heavy weight on her, she couldn't run away. So without a means of escape, she could only lecture herself in a stern mental voice instead. *Don't believe it. Don't let yourself take seriously the words of a man experienced in pillow talk.*

He probably said it to all the women who shared a bed with him—a warm token of affection, not real, not lasting emotion.

"Erin?" he said drowsily, perhaps sensing her dismay.

She had to play this just right. "I had fun too," she

murmured, turning her head away. "You've been such a fun man to know."

Knox steered the Indian into the Farmers' cul-de-sac. The motorcycle was running like a dream. When he'd paid Cass's assistant Jolly the bill that morning—the older man had been at an appointment with his rheumatologist—he'd added a couple hundred extra dollars for the care they'd taken and for the inconvenience of having to return Erin's Fiat to her.

He'd driven it home the night before when he'd left her bed.

As he'd dressed, she'd made the suggestion herself, claiming she was too sleepy to return him to the Rest Ezy. He suspected she'd wanted their protracted goodbye—the one that had started days before—to finally be over, then and there.

Parking at the curb between the two Farmer homes, Knox released the chin strap on his helmet and pinched the bridge of his nose, trying to keep a wave of exhaustion at bay. On his mattress at the motel, he'd slept in fitful starts between dreams in which he saw his father in the distance but he could never seem to reach the man, whether he was paddling on his surfboard, running down the street, or riding on the Indian. Awake hadn't been any more pleasant. He couldn't help reliving those last moments with Erin, her guarded expression, the way her big silver eyes wouldn't meet his.

His lips had brushed her warm forehead, and for a moment she'd clutched his hand. But then her fingers had slipped from his, and he'd walked away as he had from women before.

Only this time neither one of them had been

smiling.

Shit. Trying to leave behind the memory, he swung off the bike and unbuckled one of the saddlebags to retrieve the pink-wrapped gift he'd stashed there. He strolled up the walkway to Marissa and Tom's front door, wishing he could have found a way to bring flowers for Marissa, too. The tiny present was for the recent arrival.

He made a mental note to order a bouquet to be delivered later in the week for the new mom as well as a selection of beers of the world for the proud papa.

That would be easy to arrange on the road.

The metal mailbox lid squeaked as he opened it, and he slid the package inside. Then, on a second thought, he pulled it back out. Maybe it would be safer in the hands of Deanne and Rob if they were home.

Just as he approached the neighboring house, the garage door began to rise. He stood on the sidewalk and watched a big pick-up back out then come to a stop in the driveway. Rob climbed out of the driver's seat.

"Hey," he said, his expression surprised. "I didn't expect to see you."

"Yeah. Hello, Rob." Then the man's wife exited the house, and Knox raised his hand to greet her, too. "Hi, Deanne. I hear congratulations are in order. You both have a niece."

"Yep." Her friendly smile didn't convey she knew anything about his date with Erin the night before. Not a flick of an eyelash indicated she knew he'd accosted a stranger. Gone crazy over a closet of cleaning and painting supplies. Come to recognize his symptoms of grief.

And confessed to her best friend that he loved her only to hear Erin dismiss his feelings.

You've been such a fun man to know.

He cleared his throat and approached Deanne with the small present in hand. "Can I give this to you to pass on to your niece?"

She took the small box, her expression pleased. "Of course, as long as you tell me what's inside."

"A baby bracelet. I found a little jeweler on the main street in Cinnabar—"

"Finley's?"

He nodded. "They were nice enough to engrave it with her first and middle name while I waited."

Beaming, Deanne clutched the gift to her heart. "Why am I not surprised you know every girl—even a brand new one—loves jewelry?"

"Great, Brannigan," Rob complained, but in a good-natured tone, "make the rest of the brotherhood look bad."

"Hey, I saw the furniture in that little girl's room that you had a hand in crafting. That's a gift that will be handed down for generations."

Now it was Rob's turn to look pleased. "Well, if you feel that way, maybe you can help me with something."

Knox lifted a shoulder. "Sure."

The only thing on his agenda was putting miles between him and Erin and that was going to hurt no matter when he hit the road.

"This way," Rob said, leading him around the house in the direction of the rear workshop. As they entered, he indicated a beautiful wooden container sitting on a dolly. "It's a hope chest I'm scheduled to deliver today. I could use some help getting it into my truck."

The piece was incredible, with dove-tailed joints, a carved scene of a mountain home on the front, and *Alicia Faye* inscribed on the top.

Knox ghosted his fingers over the letters. "You should be doing this full-time."

"I told you we'd like to. Maybe someday."

The two of them trundled it from the workshop to the truck, then rolled it up the ramp the other man fitted to the pick-up's gate. Knox watched while Rob secured the piece with straps.

"Thanks," he said, jumping down from the bed. "All set to go."

Knox rubbed the back of his fingers against his jaw, weighing pros and cons. Then he made a swift decision.

"When your brother's over the first throes of new daddy delirium, I'd like the both of you to give me a call."

Rob's brows rose. "About?"

"I invest in ventures I find interesting." The entire thing could be managed long distance if he liked, so he'd never have to encounter Erin. "Maybe I could do something for you and Tom. *With* you and Tom."

Rob looked intrigued, but cautious. "We're very small—"

"How I like things," Knox said, "to start."

"Okay," the other man said slowly. "We'll call."

"Let me get you my contact info." He walked to the Indian to fish a card from the saddlebags.

Rob shoved it in his back pocket, but his gaze didn't leave the bike. "You never said your broken motorcycle looked like this."

"1953 Indian Chief."

"Where'd you find it?"

"In a storage locker. It belonged to my father."

"Man, I bet it has stories to tell."

"Yeah." But since it couldn't speak, he'd likely never know what possessed Colin to bequeath it to his sixth son.

Except, Knox thought now, rubbing his forehead, he'd never pumped Cass for any information he might—even unwittingly—hold. After hearing Mickey had passed on, Knox had assumed that lead was a dead end. And then he'd been distracted by yoga girl and the confusion of falling in love. But her father could know something…

Huh. He and the Indian had another stop to make before leaving the area for good.

After a firm handshake from Rob and a warm hug from Deanne, Knox turned the bike toward Mickey's Motorcycle Sales & Repair.

"I thought I'd missed you," Cass said, walking out of one of the bays as Knox pulled into the lot and parked near the office. "Bike running all right?"

"Running great."

"Saw that extra you paid," Cass said. "That wasn't necessary."

Knox waved it off, then glanced at Erin's Fiat, sitting in a space nearby. "You haven't returned it to her yet? Sorry for the trouble."

"Never trouble to look in on my girl. Jolly and I'll do it later."

Shoving his hands into his pockets, Knox hoped he wasn't going to sound like a fool. "I know it's a long shot, but do you know anything about the Indian?"

"Only a few hundred were manufactured."

"Six-hundred, actually." Knox cast a look over his shoulder at the vintage machine. "But I mean about this particular Indian. About this particular Indian and my father, Colin Brannigan."

"Well." Cass crossed his arms over his chest. "I wondered when you'd get around to asking."

Knox stared. "You know something? You...did my dad buy it from you?"

"Not me. My brother Mickey. And Colin Brannigan didn't exactly buy it from him."

"Wow." Knox stumbled back and sat sideways on the motorcycle seat. "I don't understand. Why didn't you tell me?"

"He asked me not to." Cass shrugged. "Sometime toward the end of the summer, your dad called here. Said you might come calling and, if you did, I should tell you what I knew...but only if you sought out the information."

Hell. Knox forked a hand through his hair. "Why?"

"I got the impression things might have been strained between you. Maybe he thought you wouldn't be curious."

You never take anything seriously! Bitterness crawled up Knox's throat.

"Maybe he thought you wouldn't care to know a little bit more about your dad," Cass continued.

More confused than ever, Knox frowned. "I don't get it."

"The Indian was repayment for the seed money your dad put into Mickey's business."

"Huh?"

"According to my brother, they met on a fishing trip in Alaska quite a while back."

Okay, Knox thought, that was something his dad did religiously, to the surprise of his sons. "He went every year." Finn got to accompany him once, when he was thirteen, but none of the other brothers ever got an invite.

"That's where Mickey ran into him. Your father didn't use his real name when he was on those trips— Mick discovered it later—but I guess in the course of talking, Colin offered my brother a chance to start his business."

Colin? Backing a repair shop in the middle of nowhere? Because though tourism had caught on recently, years back this area would have been quiet with a capital Q. Mogul Colin Brannigan had made a mom-and-pop style investment?

Wow.

And what was with the fake name?

"Mickey told me that over the years Colin met other people on those trips and he helped them get started on their dreams too."

Now stunned, Knox stared off into the distance, hearing Erin's voice echoing in his head. *Knox, don't you see? You give people their dreams.*

"He said you get people started in businesses as well," Cass said.

Knox's gaze shot to the other man. "He knew?"

Cass shrugged. "Seems so. A bar? Something about shoelaces? Said you do real well."

Tension pounded at Knox's temples.

"Sounded like he was real proud of you, son. And he told me he thought that you, of all his boys, would get a big kick out of owning the Indian. He hoped you would, anyway."

"God." Knox hung his head. Why hadn't Colin

spoken to him of any of this? "God, what a damn stubborn cuss."

"Failing of the gender," Cass said.

"We had a falling out. And I thought…well, at the time he made it clear he was convinced I would squander my time. My life."

"He knew you didn't."

Bands tightened around Knox's chest. *Damn stubborn cuss!* "Why wouldn't he just tell me?" Couldn't he have apologized? Though, no, Colin Brannigan never liked to admit he was wrong about anything.

Cass shrugged, then slid his hands into his coverall pockets. "A lot of men find it hard to open up their hearts and say exactly what they mean."

Knox gave a short laugh. "That sums up Colin Brannigan—at least when it comes to talking to me."

"You should learn from his mistakes."

"Right. When I want to leave a message for a son someday, I'll write a damn letter and put a stamp on it." Knox narrowed his eyes at Cass. "I could have ridden out of here without learning the truth."

"Yeah, I didn't think you'd get away so easily."

Suspicion tickled the edges of Knox's mind. "What's that supposed to mean?"

"You know…" Cass said, tilting his head to peer at the bike over Knox's shoulder, "Indian made a sidecar to go with that model. I've been trying to find you one. Getting close."

His assistant Jolly wandered out of the office as Cass mused, almost to himself, "I thought we could milk the need to work on those points for another day or two, but Jolly's a lousy fibber."

With a sudden guilty expression, his assistant

spun around and disappeared again.

Knox's jaw dropped and he aimed accusing eyes at Cass. "What? Are you saying the points were fine?"

"Well…" The older man rocked back on his heels.

"You lied to me, you forced me to stick around, so I could get a *sidecar*?"

"Simmer down, son."

Steam surely burst from Knox's ears. "Simmer down—"

"I saw the way you looked at my daughter. I saw the way she looked at you. Maybe I thought I could help by giving it a little bit of time to…bloom."

Knox put a hand to his head, trying to rub away the pain there.

"She's lonely," Cass said. "I can see that. And she works too hard so I worry. I made sure you were a decent man once I could tell she liked you."

"Not enough," Knox said, more pain piercing his head. "She doesn't like me enough. I told her…"

He blinked, then started again. "I told her…" But had he really told her anything?

His mind returned to the night before. Her room. Her bed.

He'd whispered his feelings for her, spilling them like a shameful secret instead of making an honest declaration. *Instead of opening up his heart and saying exactly what he meant.*

Instead of telling her what he wanted. Who.

Like Colin, maybe, protecting himself from rejection and hurt.

You should learn from his mistakes.

"God." Closing his eyes, he pushed the heels of his hands against his temples, hope sluicing over the pain. "I've got to make a plan. I've got to do this right."

For the first time in his life, Knox Brannigan was going to have to convince a woman his intentions were serious.

Chapter 12

Per her usual custome, Erin stood at the open door of her studio, saying goodbye to her students.

"See you next time!" she said to Connie and Debbie, two of the last to exit.

Then it was only irascible Earl Baker and his wife, Fran. Once she saw them on their way, she could go upstairs to strip her bed and wash the linens. Then they'd smell like dryer sheets instead of Knox's irresistible scent.

Surely that would make it easier for her to forget him.

"What's with the long face?" Earl demanded, pausing at the threshold before she had a chance to wish him a good day. "Isn't yoga about finding inner peace and harmony? You look like inside you is one big belly ache."

"Earl!" Fran said, shaking her head.

"What? I thought class was supposed to make us

feel better."

"How's your back now, after our fifty minutes?" Erin asked, hoping to divert him. "You seem to be moving less stiffly than when you came in."

"She's ignoring my question," Earl said to his wife. "You see that she's ignoring my question."

Fran rolled her eyes and wrapped her hand around his elbow to pull him out the door. "Give the girl some peace."

Lifting her hand to wave them on their way, Erin could only wonder if "the girl" was ever going to find some peace, now that Knox had gone. It didn't seem fair that she'd become attached to him so quickly.

Your dad and mom married after knowing each other two days.

And look how that turned out.

Just as she moved to shut the studio's door, familiar cars pulled into the parking lot. Her Fiat, with her dad behind the wheel, followed by Jolly's rusted old beater.

Okay. She blew out a long breath, then plastered on a smile as she crossed the blacktop to meet Cass. *Happy face, happy feelings*, she told herself.

And if that failed, then she could at least make an effort to hide her misery.

"Hey, Dad," she said as he climbed out of the driver's side. "Thanks so much for taking time out of your day to do this."

"Not a problem." He passed over the key fob. "Your friend paid me and Jolly extra to bring it back."

She tried to pretend a nonchalance she didn't feel. "He's on his way then?"

"Gone and back and gone again."

"Oh. Well." Gone was the operative word, right?

That's that, she thought, mentally brushing her palms together. *This time the goodbye stuck.*

"You okay, honey?"

"Fab!" she said, trying to pick up the corners of her mouth. "Just feeling a little letdown after all the baby excitement yesterday."

"Marissa and daughter doing well?"

"I called and they're both great. Tom sounded exhausted, however."

Cass chuckled. "I remember when you were born. I couldn't figure out how such a scrap of a thing could make so much noise. Your mom, however, said you were quieter than a cat. Guess motherhood made her more tolerant of that infant screeching."

Her dad always said Erin had been born with the loudest pair of lungs in Central California. But maybe not the sharpest brain, because she heard herself asking about Suzie Cassidy, even though she already knew the answer.

"You haven't heard from her, Dad?"

"Ah, Erin." He shook his head. "No birthday card this year?"

She half-smiled. "You know me so well."

"I do. I can see when you're sad. I can see too, when you're brimming with happy—like yesterday."

"It was special, with Elizabeth Erin coming to town."

"Is that all? What about the other newcomer to the area? He seemed to put stars in your eyes."

Erin glanced away. "It doesn't matter. Like you said, he's gone." Proving once again how easy she was to leave behind.

"Really?" Cass cocked his head. "I think I recognize the purr of that engine."

Then she heard it too, the thrum of a motorcycle. Her eyes widened as Knox turned in, his black and chrome Indian glinting in the sun. He came to a stop, his booted feet braced on the blacktop as he unclipped his helmet. Then he was combing a hand through his disordered hair, his gaze never leaving hers.

Her body flashed hot, cold, hot.

She swallowed, trying to ease her dry mouth as he hung the helmet on his handlebars and started toward her. *Game face*, she told herself, *get your game face on.*

"I didn't expect to see you!" she called out as he approached. *Ever again.* Her gaze dropped from his dark eyes to his powerful torso, the hard, sculpted muscles that she'd run her hands over the night before.

She tucked her arms close to her sides to make sure she didn't forget herself and reach for him again. "What, uh, brings you here?"

Instead of answering, he nodded at her dad. "Cass. I didn't think I'd see you again quite so soon."

"I didn't think I'd see you again at all," Erin muttered. How many more goodbyes could she take without completely losing it?

Knox turned to her. "What's that, darlin'?"

"I'm only wondering about your latest reappearance." She glanced at him, but then had to look away. He was studying her with an intensity she found unnerving. "I can't think why you've turned up here."

Gah. She sounded as grumpy as old Earl.

"I left something undone," Knox said.

Her gaze flew to his face. "Not that stupid wall again."

He grimaced. "The wall's for another time. Now I'm here because…" He rubbed the back of his neck in seeming frustration. "Hell, I never have trouble with words. Then you came along, Erin, and upended me."

She blinked. Because he'd upended her, too. Her life had been disciplined, ordered, safe for six long years. Until meeting him.

It was getting behind Knox for that motorcycle ride, she decided, that had been the turning point. Yes, she'd found the experience exhilarating at the time, but the serenity she'd felt sitting behind him had been deceptive. Erin had given up control that day.

She'd been holding onto him instead of having her own hands on the steering wheel of her life.

Now he shot a look at Cass, before redirecting his gaze to her. "Maybe we could go inside…"

"Don't mind me," her father said, jovial as all get out.

Knox let out a short laugh. "I thought I'd been vetted," he said, mysteriously. Then he blew out a breath and shifted to address Erin again. "Okay. Here's the thing…"

He seemed to go speechless once more. And maybe a touch uncertain, which was an unusual state of being for mai tai-making, ladies-of-all-sizes-pleasing Knox Brannigan. His hand shoved through his hair again, and when he let it drop, she didn't think. She picked it up and inspected his injuries from the utility knife.

"You took off the bandages," she said, frowning at the cuts, which appeared to be healing.

He curled his fingers around hers. "Erin, I came back to tell you I'm in love with you."

She froze, her gaze on their joined hands. "I...*what*?"

"I've fallen in love with you."

Her head lifted, and she glanced around, wondering if she'd been transported to some other world. But there was her studio behind her, and Cass, and Jolly, and Knox Brannigan, looking at her without a trace of his usual good humor or charm.

He was sincere.

She tried pulling away from him. His hold tightened.

"You can't," she said.

Now he half-smiled. "Turns out I can. Took me a while to recognize it myself." He brought their hands to his mouth and kissed her fingers.

"It fills me up, Erin. I'm overflowing with it."

There was a high whine in her ears. She looked at her dad, the only anchor she'd ever known. The only one who'd loved her enough to never leave her.

"I can't..." Pressure built behind the back of her eyes. "How do I know..."

"I'm aware I have a reputation for not taking things seriously—"

"Of course you take things seriously," she snapped.

That earned her another little smile. "And I said I was all fun-and-games."

"You're so much more than that."

"Then can I hope..." He inhaled a deep breath. "Then can I hope you're in love with me, too?"

She stared at him a moment before the answer boomed in her head.

Yes.

The knowledge of it was just...there, lodged

inside her heart like a precious treasure waiting to be found. *Yes.* She put her free hand over her eyes. *Gah!* Did she have no sense of self-preservation at all?

When had she been so foolish as to fall in love with Knox Brannigan?

Probably at first sight, she thought miserably. Her birthday night at the Moonstone Café when, wearing that devilish smile and oozing confident charm, he'd invited her to sit down.

Even though she'd already pegged him as the type who would never get tied down.

"Baby," he whispered now. "You're killing me here."

And he looked in pain, she thought, as she took her hand from her eyes.

"I…I am in love with you," she said, because she found she never, ever wanted to cause him hurt.

"God." He yanked her into his arms and buried his face in her hair. She could feel him tremble against her. "You don't know how glad I am to hear you say that."

"But I don't know…" A hot tear ran down her face. "I still don't know…"

"What, baby?" He set her away from him and looked into her eyes. "What's got you worried?"

"How can we know that it's really real? That it will last?"

He brushed her hair off her forehead and then erased the lone tear with the edge of his thumb. "Well, when I talked about you to my brother Luke, he said—"

"Wait. You told your brother about me?" It shot a thrill of secret pleasure through her.

"I did." Knox cupped her face between his big

hands. "And he told me to believe in myself. To trust my own judgment."

Erin thought of her mother's defection, of the big blunder that had been Wylie. She couldn't afford to make another mistake. Being left again would hurt. Being left by Knox Brannigan would crush her. "I don't know that I can do that. Trust myself."

"Oh, baby." He leaned forward to press a kiss to her forehead. "I understand."

And she thought he probably did. Another tear ran down her cheek, and he caught this one too and rubbed it into her hot skin. "Luke's fiancée says something else."

"What?"

"She says you have to trust and believe in the other person," Knox said. "So…"

"So…" Erin echoed.

He inhaled a long breath. "Can you do that? Can you trust and believe in me?"

She stared into his face, made even more impossibly handsome by the tenderness of his intent expression. It said, clear as day, that he would make her his world if she let him.

And love for him expanded inside her, filling her up too, filling her from the bottom of her toes to the top of her head, to then overflow in another pair of tears. Yes, she could trust. Yes, she could believe.

She could be Knox Brannigan's love, and he could be hers.

"Okay," she said. "Yes. I can do that. I can do that for sure."

"In that case…" He withdrew his phone.

"You're going to make a call?" A kiss to seal the deal would be better.

He grinned at her. "I'm going to call in some of the troops."

Before she could fathom what he was getting at, another vehicle pulled into her parking area. Tom's huge truck, with Tom driving and Deanne riding shotgun. They must have been waiting nearby for Knox's text.

"What's going on?" Erin asked.

Taking her hand, he drew her toward the big vehicle. "Now close your eyes."

"What?"

"Just do it!" Deanne yelled through her open window.

"Trust me," Knox whispered in her ear.

"All right." She obediently let her lashes drift down.

"She'll peek," Deanne yelled again.

Chuckling, Knox covered Erin's eyes with his palm.

Mysterious sounds came from the direction of the truck. She heard a grunt or two and footsteps—her dad and Jolly she guessed—but Knox didn't leave her side.

Erin found herself smiling, even in the dark as she was, because charming, handsome, wonderful Knox Brannigan was her man! She leaned against him, and he kissed the top of her head.

"Just another moment or two."

"I'm trying to be patient."

He kissed her again. "Okay. Now I'm just going to tell you, darlin', that tickets to Paris or even a pony would have been much easier." Then he lifted his hand away.

Standing in front of Erin was an old-fashioned

claw-foot tub. And inside the tub were flowers. Dozens and dozens and dozens arranged in vases that completely packed the space so that it was brimming with tulips and roses and daffodils and daisies. Their perfume reached her on the next gust of breeze.

A bathtub filled with flowers.

"Where did you get all these?" she asked, reaching out to touch a delicate curled petal.

"The Cinnabar, California florists are now my new best friends," he said lightly, but he was looking at her with that tender-solemn gaze once again.

She was vaguely aware that the others were ranged around them—Deanne definitely wouldn't want to miss this show—but Erin only saw the beautiful display and the man she loved.

"I…what exactly is this, Knox?"

"Remember how you told me I give people their dreams? You're the most important person whose dream I want to fulfill."

"Me." Her heart started beating faster and faster.

"You," he said. "So here's the bathtub, and the flowers, and…" he reached into his pocket and pulled out a small velvet box and popped open the top. "The ring."

Erin heard Deanne gasp, but she only looked away from the beautiful gem to gaze into Knox's face. "It's a moonstone," she said.

"Surrounded by diamonds that shine like your eyes. It will always remind me of the night we met."

"The night we fell in love."

His huge smile heated her like the sun. "Will you marry me, Erin?"

She threw herself into his arms. "Only like a thousand million times."

Laughing, he swung her around, but she was already dizzy with love and joy. "I'll take that," he said. "And I'm taking you and keeping you for the rest of our lives."

Epilogue

—⟫⟪—

Erin slipped through the front door of the bar known as The Wake in Santa Monica, California. Helium-filled heart-shaped balloons kissed the ceiling. The floor was strewn with red, white, and silver confetti. Cupids of red foil cardboard hung over the tables and a big banner strung over the bar wished the customers a *Very Happy Valentine's Day!*

The place was romantically low-lit and already packed with customers. Through the speakers Celine Dion was singing "The Power of Love." Knox likely wanted to kill somebody over that particular jukebox pick.

She kept to the shadows because she didn't see her fiancé behind the bar and because, truth be told, she'd gotten a little nervous when they'd spent time apart. He was winding down his work at The Wake— they were hiring a replacement bartender—but tonight would be busy, and so he'd headed from Cinnabar to

Santa Monica a few days prior to get some work done on his beachside house and then take the February 14th shift.

But the plan was for Knox to relocate permanently ASAP. He said he wanted to be near his yoga girl.

Erin pressed damp palms to her red dress. Underneath the sleek knit she wore risqué red little-nothings, including a garter belt and sheer stockings. The high heels on her feet were killer red and actual killers—already her toes were shrieking, and she couldn't wait to slip them off. But they were the kind of shoes that told a man what his woman had been thinking about.

Then she saw him come out from the back, a rack of clean glassware in his hands. He wore dark jeans and a red button-down shirt, the cuffs rolled up to the elbows. A patron seated on a stool pulled up to the bar made a remark that caused Knox to laugh, his teeth flashing white.

She waited where she was for a stool to become free. Then, on a deep breath, she wound through the tables to approach the bar. Knox stood with his back to her and for a moment she recalled that worst-case scenario she'd once imagined in the restaurant at the spa-resort. What if when he turned there wasn't a welcome in his expression?

Their relationship had developed so quickly. But the mutual physical attraction had been obvious from the first and they'd found themselves quickly sharing their inner selves too. Everyone she knew who knew Knox as well thought they were an excellent match—and she had to agree. His rebel's confidence rubbed off on her. Her trust in his love allowed him to see a deeper side of himself.

They each made the other more.

Or, she thought, with another nervous flutter in her stomach, they *had* made each other more. But it had been five days without talking to him in person, touching him skin-to-skin, seeing his feelings for her written all over his face.

Erin stood behind the barstool when Knox glanced over his shoulder. Their gazes met.

Love blazed in his eyes, hot enough that she wobbled a little on her heels and had to clutch the bar with her hand for support.

"Hey," he said, turning. Smiling. His palm pressed against his chest. "Is there an airport nearby, or is that my heart taking off?"

Oh, God, she loved this man.

Then he hurried along the bar, ducking beneath the hinged opening. She met him halfway, and they embraced, oblivious to anyone around them. His mouth met hers, and the kiss assuaged the last of her nerves.

He lifted his head, smiling down at her. "How are you?"

"Well, I've been a little under the weather."

"What?" His brows came together in concern.

"Yes," she said, kissing the underside of his square chin. "My doctor says I've been lacking Vitamin U."

Laughing, he pushed her a little away. "Have you been studying pick-up lines?"

"Just practicing in case I ever have to go after fresh meat again."

"Never," he said, emphatic. "You're all mine. Only mine. And I'm only yours."

They kissed again.

"And because I'm so grateful for that," he murmured against her mouth, "and because it's Valentine's Day…" From his pocket he withdrew a small square box.

"Knox!" She smiled at him. "You'll spoil me."

"Get used to it." He flipped open the top to show her moonstone and diamond earrings, a match to her engagement ring.

"Oh." She quickly changed out the simple hoops she was wearing for the new jewelry. "Pretty?"

With his hand on her chin, he tilted her face this way and that. "Beautiful. I had no idea that angels could fly so low."

Erin felt herself blush as she went on tiptoe to kiss him again and then whisper in his ear, "As for your Valentine's presents…I left one at your house when I stopped there to change. The other gifts…well, you'll find them when you unwrap me later."

Clutching her tighter, Knox groaned. "All right, lady, you've officially made the rest of my shift torture. Come sit down. I need to put the bar between us before I give in to temptation and race out with you over my shoulder."

She slid onto the empty stool and he went back to making drinks. Content just to watch him, she sipped at the glass of wine he slid in front of her and listened to the love songs playing over the speakers.

"You've got a dreamy look in your eyes," he said, stopping in front of her.

"That kind of night, I guess."

He reached out to take her hand. "Cass said a birthday card finally showed up for you from your mom."

Her eyebrows rose. "You talked to my dad?"

"Just checking in. How come you didn't tell me about it?"

Erin shrugged. "It doesn't seem quite so important now." She squeezed his hand. "I have my dad, my friends, I have you."

"You do. You always will." He plucked a maraschino cherry from the tray of bar garnishes and popped it into his mouth. Chewed. "Oh, and I finally spoke with Finn over the phone."

She knew Knox had called each of his older brothers to announce his and Erin's engagement and to explain about his varied business pursuits that he'd kept secret from them. They'd expressed interest and admiration, but most of all they'd assured him that they cared about him no matter whether he invested in shoelaces and custom furniture businesses or spent the rest of his life surfing and slinging drinks.

That response had pleased him to no end.

But his younger brother had proved difficult to reach outside of brief emails recently, making Knox worry a little. She was glad to hear they'd made contact.

"How is he?"

"Sounds great, and he wanted me to pass on his sympathy to you for taking me on." Knox grinned. "But with the Brannigan brothers falling like dominoes, we spent most of the conversation making bets on which one will topple next."

"Are you going to tell me who you think is the most likely candidate?"

"A brother who's not as lucky as me, because I found the best and most beautiful girl in the world."

Her eyebrows rose. "Another pick-up line?"

"Straight from the depths of my heart, baby," Knox said, with that tender expression on his face that scrambled her pulse and made her melt all over. "Straight from the very depths of my heart."

THE END

—➤➤◀◀←—

Also by Christie Ridgway

<u>Rock Royalty Series</u>
Light My Fire (#1)
Love Her Madly (#2)
Break on Through (#3)
Touch Me (#4)
Wishful Sinful (#5)
Wild Child (#6)
Who Do You Love (# 7) *Coming soon!*

<u>Billionaire's Beach Series</u>
Take Me Tender (#1)
Take Me Forever (#2)
Take Me Home (#3)
The Scandal (#4)
The Seduction (#5) *Coming soon!*
The Secret (#6) *Coming soon!*

—➤➤◀◀←—

About The Author

Christie Ridgway is the author of over forty-five novels of contemporary romance. All her books are both sexy and emotional and tell about heroes and heroines who learn to believe in the power of love. A *USA Today* bestseller, Christie is a six-time RITA finalist and has won best contemporary romance of the year and career achievement awards from *Romantic Times Book Reviews*.

A native of California, Christie now resides in the southern part of the state with her family. Inspired by the beaches, mountains, and cities that surround her, she writes tales of sunny days and steamy nights. For a complete list of books, excerpts, and news on the latest going on with Christie:

Visit Christie's Website:
www. christieridgway.net

Join Christie on Facebook:
www.facebook.com/christieridgway

Follow Christie on Twitter:
http://www.twitter.com/christieridgway

Made in the USA
Las Vegas, NV
20 April 2023

70810024R00132